STRANGE RITUALS

Pushing through the crowd, Horne spotted brawny Fred Babcock and his swarthy opponent. The two men faced one another as they revolved in a circle, dipping and weaving, bodies smeared with dirt.

Horne saw that the contest was not the usual bareknuckle fight. Each man had his left hand tied behind his back and the right hand lashed to a cudgel, a thick piece of wood with a hollow base to accommodate the fist and carved to resemble clenched fingers. The combatants' feet were bare except for a leather strap holding a blade to the right ankle.

Circling Babcock, the pirate jabbed with the wooden fist, at the same time twisting the scythe-like blade jutting from his foot. Excited voices rose from the spectators, the majority of men cheering for the Malagasy, calling his name— Katu—and urging him to kill the *topiwallah,* a foreigner.

The pirate steadied himself from a blow in the stomach, quickly bringing his fist down sideways. The edge of the carved fingers drew a line of scarlet across Babcock's bare shoulder.

Lowering his head, Babcock charged forward like a bull.

Katu stepped aside, twisting his right foot to raise the blade toward Babcock's stomach, but Babcock dived sideways.

Continuing to circle, Katu punched the wooden fist to block Babcock's path. Babcock dodged again and drove his left knee into Katu's groin. As the pirate doubled over in pain, Babcock grabbed him by his hair, simultaneously raising his right ankle to drive his throat onto the blade. . . .

By the same author

THE WAR CHEST
THE BOMBAY MARINES

CHINA FLYER

An Adam Horne Adventure

Porter Hill

BERKLEY BOOKS, NEW YORK

CHINA FLYER

A Berkley Book / published by arrangement with
Walker Publishing Company, Inc.

PRINTING HISTORY
Walker and Company hardcover edition published in 1988
Berkley mass-market edition / March 2001

The Penguin Putnam Inc. World Wide Web site address is
http://www.penguinputnam.com

ISBN: 0-425-17882-X

BERKLEY®
Berkley Books are published by The Berkley Publishing Group,
a division of Penguin Putnam Inc., 375 Hudson Street,
New York, New York 10014.
BERKLEY and the "B" design
are trademarks belonging to Penguin Putnam Inc.

PRINTED IN THE UNITED STATES OF AMERICA

10 9 8 7 6 5 4 3 2 1

*Dedicated to
Christopher Vaughn*

CONTENTS

THE EAST INDIA COMPANY

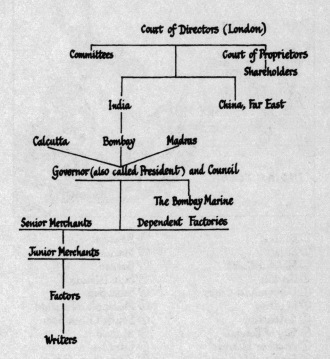

Court of Directors (London)

Committees   Court of Proprietors
Shareholders

India   China, Far East

Calcutta   Bombay   Madras

Governor (also called President) and Council

The Bombay Marine

Senior Merchants   Dependent Factories

Junior Merchants

Factors

Writers

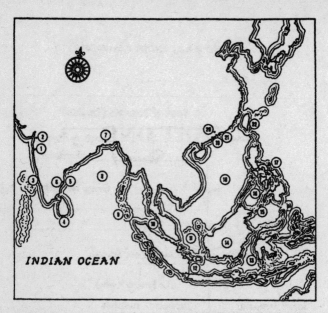

① Bombay	⑫ Bantam
② Surat	⑬ Macassar
③ Malabar Coast	⑭ Borneo
④ Ceylon	⑮ Sulu Islands
⑤ Coromandel Coast	⑯ Sulu Sea
⑥ Madras	⑰ Philippine Islands
⑦ Calcutta	⑱ South China Sea
⑧ Bay of Bengal	⑲ Macao
⑨ Nicobar Islands	⑳ Canton
⑩ Strait of Malacca	㉑ Kam-Sing-Moon
⑪ Malaysia	㉒ Formosa

PART ONE
The Scent

1

Rose Cottage

Bombay Marine Captain Adam Horne shifted uncomfortably on the edge of the dainty parlour chair placed to face the divan with its recumbent figure. Forcing himself to ignore his Commander-in-Chief's frail condition, he tried to concentrate on the older man's explanation for summoning him to the homely cottage in Bombay's Old Church Quarter. Commodore Watson held a damp cloth to his mottled pate as he talked, gasping out the words.

"I was leaving my chambers yesterday in Bombay Castle . . . feeling like a poxy camel . . . when Governor Spencer stopped me in the courtyard . . . and . . . and . . . gave me the news about—" Watson winced with obvious discomfort, then proceeded painfully. "—gave me news about a Company man disappearing from Fort St. George and—"

Horne watched as Watson paused to gulp some water. He wondered if he should insist that his chief stop talking until he felt better. Why should the old walrus sacrifice his health for the Honourable East India Company? Commodore Watson shouldered more than his share of responsibilities as Commander-in-Chief of the Company's

3

private naval force, the Bombay Marine; there was no need for him to keep going while on his sick bed.

Watson struggled on. "Governor Spencer's named you, Horne, to sail to Madras to find the missing fellow."

Horne forgot his concern for his superior's health. "Governor Spencer orders *me* to Madras, sir?" he asked.

Watson's suety face flushed as he rose from the pillows, rasping with sudden irritation, "Dash it, Horne! How else can you pick up the scent of a man gone missing? You can't play bloodhound from this side of the blasted country."

"No, sir. Of course not, sir." Horne remained sitting stiffly on the edge of his chair, his hat on his knee. The outburst told him that Watson's condition might not be as fatal as he had feared.

Watson sank back on the divan. "True," he admitted, "the Governor ordered silence about your last trip to Madras. But now it seems they're sending you to Fort St. George in broad daylight. In an official capacity." He closed his eyes. "The Lord only knows what skulduggery they want you to do this time."

It was no secret that Commodore Watson disapproved of the East India Company's use of their Bombay Marine, and especially of Horne's rag-tag squadron of ex-convicts. Horne viewed his deployment more realistically: the Honourable East India Company hired him to keep trading routes open, waters free of pirates and strife, enabling the Company to remain the largest, richest trading company in the world. Surely that made the Bombay Marine virtually mercenaries. He did not complain when he was treated as such.

He waited silently, feeling uncomfortably hot in his blue and gold uniform, with its silk shirt tight around his neck and breeches snug above the gleaming black horse-leather boots. The wide rattan sweeps of a ceiling fan pulled by the punkahwallah in a far corner did little to ease the room's temperature.

The tempting aroma of cooking drifted through the cottage—roasting chicken, baking bread, stewing apples. Looking around the cluttered parlour, he considered he might very well be in England. The furnishings, the smells from the kitchen, even the small house's name— Rose Cottage—suggested a way of life far removed from India. Yet he knew that outside the front door a narrow street led down to a thoroughfare busy with cedarwood palanquins, plodding elephants painted with indigo, women running behind bullocks with cupped hands to catch dung to burn as fuel in their hovels.

Watson drank some more water and set down the posy-painted tumbler, asking weakly, "What was I saying, Horne, before you interrupted me?"

"You were telling me, sir, about a Company employee disappearing from Madras."

"Ah, yes. George Fanshaw."

Horne made a note of the man's name.

Watson resumed dabbing his forehead with the wet cloth. "George Fanshaw's a purchasing agent. He buys cotton for merchants back in England. Less than three months ago he disappeared from Fort St. George. The coffers came up short around the same time. Madras doesn't think Fanshaw absconded to England with the money. Spencer has received word that Pigot and Vansittart want you to investigate a trail leading somewhere else."

The power of the Honorable East India Company—in India, in 1762—was divided between three governors, Spencer of Bombay, Pigot of Madras, Vansittart of Bengal. In the past, Commodore Watson had been the buffer between Horne and the three governors, relaying their orders, passing on as many details as the governors allowed him to divulge, and occasionally telling Horne more than he was supposed to by using insinuation or supposedly irrelevant asides. Had the governors again muzzled Watson, leaving the Marines to hear the full facts at a later date from a senior source, even from one of the governors himself?

Horne tried for a few nuggets. "Sir, do the governors believe George Fanshaw's still in India?"

"You'll receive full details when you reach Madras," came the grumpy reply.

Evidently there would be no hints during this meeting.

Stifling a cough, Watson explained, "You sail as soon as the *Huma* is seaworthy, Horne."

The name took a few moments to penetrate Horne's thoughts.

"The *Huma*, sir?"

The stubble glistened on Watson's chin, his lips parting in a smile. "Aye, Horne. The *Huma*. The Company's given you your flying bird."

"The governors granted the Marine the *Huma* as a prize, sir?"

"Your full command's waiting aboard ship. You'll know what you need to know at the time."

"But, sir. With all due respect, sir—"

Horne stopped. Either Watson was being deliberately evasive or he felt too ill to discuss the mission at length. Whatever the reason, there was no point in pursuing the matter.

Tempering his excitement, he replied honestly, "My gratitude, sir."

Watson had turned his mind to more practical details. "Do you know where to find your men, Horne?"

"Yes, sir." Horne's excitement clouded. "I do, sir."

"What's the problem? You sound hesitant."

Horne did not want to divulge to Watson where his

men were at this hour. Bareknuckle fighting was against Company regulations, forbidden for both civilian and military employees, even in sport. Nor did he want to confess that he himself—much to his shame—might have been attending the bareknuckle match at this very moment if Watson had not summoned him to Rose Cottage.

Horne's reticence piqued Watson's curiosity. His bushy eyebrows knitted as he turned his head on the pillows, asking, "Are you certain you know where to find your men, Horne?"

"Yes, sir," answered Horne. "I'm in regular contact with my Marines as well as the men who served as crew aboard the *Huma*, sir."

Watson's jowls puffed. "Then round up all the devils, Horne. The *Huma*'s being provisioned at this very hour and—"

A cough silenced him. He struggled to raise himself, groping for his tumbler of water, the other hand grasping at his throat.

Horne sprang to his feet.

At the same moment, a diminutive woman in a lace bonnet and fluttering shawl hurried into the parlour.

Watson waved away his wife, complaining, "Dash it, woman. Don't coddle me. I'm fine. I'm fine."

Mrs. Watson turned her kind face to Adam Horne. "Excuse me, Captain Horne, but the Commodore must rest."

"Of course, Mrs. Watson. By all means, ma'am."

"But you're welcome to come back and join us at table if the Commodore—" Her voice trailed off as she looked for confirmation from her husband.

Horne smelled the roast chicken and baking apples. The idea of a crusty English loaf, rather than another pile of Indian *chapatis*, greatly tempted him to seize upon the kind lady's invitation. But glancing at Watson and seeing his grimace, he quickly answered, "Thank you, ma'am, but I have pressing duties to attend to."

From his couch, Watson rasped, "Take your last look at me, Horne. I'll be six feet under the earth when you return to Bombay."

Horne refrained from joining Mrs. Watson in chiding the Commodore for his pessimism. Yet, leaving Rose Cottage, he wondered how serious the man's condition really was.

"What a nice young man Captain Horne is, dear."

"A cold-hearted rogue."

"Perhaps he needs a wife to mellow him."

"Adam Horne was betrothed to marry a young lady in London."

"And he absconded? Oh dear!"

"No, no. A band of hooligans set upon the poor lass one night in Covent Garden and murdered her in cold blood. That's why Horne came out to India. Heartbroken and bitter."

"How dreadful. That must be the reason he has such sad brown eyes."

Mrs. Watson sent her Tamil servant to pull the parlour shutters, darkening the small room in an attempt to help her husband take a nap. The Commodore refused to see Dr. Young who served the European community in Bombay, insisting that his sickness was no more than a mild bout of *coup de soleil*. Yet he was too weak to go to his office at Bombay Castle, or even to dress to receive Adam Horne. Her husband's lack of energy troubled her; he was not a person to lie around the house, definitely not a man to receive subordinates in such an informal manner. She worried that his history of gin drinking might be taking some toll on his health.

Working on a square of embroidery as she sat by her husband's divan, she said, "Dear, you should have insisted that Captain Horne join us for dinner. We always have more than enough food."

Watson jerked awake. "Hmmm? What's that?"

"Nothing, dear. Nothing. Just me chattering."

Mrs. Watson went on with her needlework, remembering that her niece would soon be arriving from England. As she pictured the spirited young lady, her thoughts returned to Adam Horne; perhaps she should give a small reception where two young people could meet without either of them suspecting they were being foisted upon one another. If anybody could pull the dashing young Marine captain out of his shell it would be Emily Harkness.

2

Fist of Oak

Adam Horne passed the row of East India Company
warehouses lining the Bombay waterfront and hurried
across a rope and wood footbridge connecting the dock-
yards to the native bazaar built on the marshlands. The
sun was blazing high in the sky and Horne felt the heat
prickle through his woollen uniform. As he stepped from
the footbridge onto the embankment, he longed to rip
open the gold buttons and free himself from the high-
collared jacket, the stifling shirt and restricting waistband.
A meeting with Commodore Watson was one of the rare
times in Marine service when he donned the heavy frock-
coat and breeches copied from the officer's dress of His
Majesty's Royal Navy. Still, he would not have to endure
the discomfort for much longer. Soon he would be shirt-
less, wearing *dungri* breeches, standing barefoot on the
quarterdeck of the *Huma* and inhaling raw salty air, and
meanwhile he was in a hurry.

Despite his disapproval of today's fight between his
Marine, Fred Babcock, and an Asian seaman, Horne did
not want to miss the match. He frowned inwardly as he
remembered how Babcock had become involved in the

challenge at a waterfront beer shop. He had been arguing about bareknuckle fighting, boasting that the English were champions of all pugilists. The other men in the beer shop had been seamen off a Malagasy raiding boat. One of the raiders had challenged the loud-mouthed Babcock to a fight, and Horne had no power on shore to prevent the fight from taking place.

The harbour marketplace was crowded with hawking pedlars, herdsmen in brightly coloured headdresses, dhoolie bearers carrying veiled women peering through curtains. Horne moved through the din of shrill voices and jangling bells, momentarily forgetting about Fred Babcock's fight as he mulled over the meeting he had left a few minutes ago at Rose Cottage.

Elated at being granted the *Huma*, Horne wondered if he would have command of the frigate merely to sail to Madras. Would it now be his official command?

And what about the mission? Would there be sealed orders aboard ship disclosing more details, or would he have to wait until Madras to hear where the Governors suspected their missing employee might have fled? The man must have disappeared with a great deal of money for the Governors to be sending the Bombay Marine after him.

First, though, there was work to accomplish here in port. The *Huma* was being provisioned at this very moment, Watson had explained. It was therefore vital to ensure that there was no cheating. A baker's dozen might be thirteen, but a naval storeman's dozen too often counted eleven, ten, nine . . .

The sound of wailing recalled Horne to his surroundings.

To his left, he saw a field stretching between the tented bazaar stalls and a clay hovel. In the centre, a circle of people sat cross-legged around a cluster of flopping vultures. Looking more closely and seeing that the vultures were fighting over—pulling apart—a human corpse, Horne realized he was witnessing a Parsi funeral.

Parsis were Indians who believed that to bury their dead in the earth—or to cremate a body by fire or inter it in the sea—was to defile those earthly elements with carrion. The Parsi mourners held one another's hands as they sat around the funeral altar, chanting prayers as the vultures voraciously tore apart the decayed flesh, the birds gorging themselves on the human feast, flopping away when they were glutted.

Horne quickened his pace, checking his disapproval of the Indian tradition as he remembered how the Parsis criticised Europeans for burying their dead in the earth. Did it really matter whether a body was eaten by vultures or by worms?

By association, his thoughts returned to Commodore Watson's remarks about being dead and buried when Horne returned from Madras.

Was Watson really so ill? If so, what was the cause? He had not seemed feverish, or no more than Horne himself in this stifling weather. In this woollen frock-coat.

Horne thought of the English world which the Watsons had recreated in India, the cosy nest they had built in the Old Church quarters, with its rural British atmosphere and homely smells. Horne himself had been in India for how long? Eight years. How European had he remained? Had he become easternised without noticing the changes in himself? His rooms near Bombay Castle were as simple as the cell of a hermit priest; no more than a place to sleep, a station to await the next command.

His commands had been few: first aboard the *Eclipse* which had been destroyed in a storm off the Coromandel Coast; latterly on the *Huma*, the frigate he had captured from pirates in the past year. Neither ship had afforded him the luxuries enjoyed by the officers of His Majesty's Navy. But, then, he was not desirous of luxury; he had abandoned households of servants back home in England. He had not tried to replace them in India, and certainly never at sea.

Reaching the Buddhist shrine he had been told to look for as a landmark, Horne turned into a deserted alleyway. As he moved farther into the dark shadows, he rested one hand on the hilt of his sword. The golden buttons fronting his jacket would melt down very nicely for some young Hindu bride's dowry; the glittering epaulets on his shoulders would fetch many rupees in the Thieves' Market.

Emerging at the alley's far end, he spotted the large shed with the conical straw roof where the fight was supposedly being fought. The low plank door stood ajar and, as Horne approached, he heard whistles and the babble of excited voices.

Pausing to prime his flintlock, he tucked the pistol into his waistband, then removed his hat to stoop and pass through the low doorway.

Horne resumed his full height inside the large barn, smelling the redolence of sweet straw intermixed with the stench of rancid perspiration. As his eyes adjusted to the faint light filtering through a hole in the roof, he appraised the crowd gathered in the middle of the dirt floor, the majority of the men being half-naked Asians with dhotties twisted around their loins and turbans knotted on their heads. Jabbering like noisy birds in a cage, the tawny-skinned men craned their necks to see the activity in the center of the shed.

Pushing through the crowd, Horne spotted brawny Fred Babcock and his swarthy opponent. The two men faced one another as they revolved in a circle, dipping and weaving, bodies smeared with dirt.

As Horne edged closer, he saw that the contest was not the usual bareknuckle fight he had expected. The Asian had obviously chosen a local form of combat.

Each man had his left hand tied behind his back and the right hand lashed to a cudgel, a thick piece of wood with a hollow base to accommodate the fist and carved to resemble clenched fingers. The combatants' feet were bare except for a leather strap holding a blade to the right ankle.

Watching the fighters as they jabbed the air with their fists and kicked their ankle blades at one another, Horne understood why many Indians believed that this sport was the forerunner of cockfighting. Afghani in origin, the club-and-blade contest had been brought to India by Moghul conquerers in the sixteenth century, when their fourteen-year-old ruler, Akbar, had ordered such matches to be held in Delhi between Hindu captives, to decide their fate.

Despite its historic origins, Horne's first instinct was to stop the match. It was not sport. It was blood lust. The ankle blades were sharply honed, the hand cudgels lethal weapons. The men might maim or kill one another.

Circling Babcock, the pirate jabbed with the wooden fist, at the same time twisting the scythe-like blade jutting from his foot. Excited voices rose from the spectators, the majority of men cheering for the Malagasy, calling his name—Katu—and urging him to kill the *topiwallah*, a foreigner.

A few natives cheered for Babcock, but his loudest support came from the small clutch of Marines standing across on the opposite side of the circle from Horne. Jingee, the delicately-boned Tamil, excitedly wagged his white-turbanned head, shouting like a man twice his size. Kiro bellowed in his native Japanese, making cutting and chopping movements with his hands as if he himself were fighting the pirate. Dirk Groot jabbered excitedly in a mixture of Dutch and English, his brilliant blue eyes following the two men inside the circle of noisy spectators.

The only Marine who visibly disapproved of the match was the African, Jud, his black face scowling and wincing as the men pummelled each other.

Horne turned from his men back to the fight.

The pirate steadied himself from a blow in the stomach, quickly bringing his fist down sideways. The edge of the carved fingers drew a line of scarlet across Babcock's bare shoulder.

Lowering his head, Babcock charged forward like a bull.

Katu stepped aside, twisting his right foot to raise the blade toward Babcock's stomach.

Babcock dived sideways.

Continuing to circle, Katu punched the wooden fist to block Babcock's path.

Horne saw the quick movement and knew that the oak fist could crack Babcock's skull, but, spotting the obstacle himself, Babcock dodged again and drove his left knee into Katu's groin. As the pirate doubled over in pain, Babcock grabbed him by his greasy shanks of hair, simultaneously raising his right ankle to drive his throat onto the blade.

At that moment a blast rent the air.

"Enough!" Horne boomed over the rabble's cheers and catcalls.

Babcock paused in his attack, gaping at Horne who was holding a smoking flintlock in one hand.

The pirate saw Babcock hesitate and, falling back, raised his right foot to slice open his stomach.

Horne had anticipated the action. Flourishing his

sword, he jabbed at the man's throat, driving him to the ground and thundering, "I ordered *stop!*"

Keeping his eyes on the Malagasy seaman, he shouted, "Babcock, report to the *Huma* immediately!"

"But, Horne—"

"Do as I say, Babcock. Report to the *Huma*."

Raising his voice, Horne called to the surrounding group, "All of you. Out of here. Go."

The uniform might be stifling, he thought, but seeing the crowd begin to disperse, he realised that the frock-coat's blue-and-gold magnificence was recognised as a symbol of unquestionable authority.

He pointed at the four Marines, adding for good measure, "What are you men gawking at? I'm talking to all of you. Out!"

Jingee the Tamil's dark eyes were large and alert under his white turban. "Leave and go to the . . . *Huma*, Captain sahib? Our old ship?"

"That's what I said." Horne pointed at the doorway. "Now out of here, all of you, before some Company snoop comes along and we have to answer to Commodore Watson for this fight."

Dirk Groot, the Dutchman, asked, "Do we have a new command, *schipper?*"

"You won't have anything if you're all thrown back into Bombay prison for attending illegal assemblies."

Horne noticed a group of Malagasy seamen loitering beyond the low doorway. Hand on the hilt of his sword, he moved outside to disperse them before his men emerged from the barn. The last thing he wanted was for the Malagasies to try and settle the score in a grudge fight arranged for a later hour, in another part of town.

3

The *Huma*

A strong wind off the Malabar Coast laid the *Huma* over as her trimmed sails caught the gust. From the quarter-deck Horne studied the distant mountains of the mainland and wondered if a morning mist was making the jagged range hazy. Or were his eyes tired after three sleepless days and nights preparing to leave Bombay? Having reasoned that he could sleep once the frigate was under way, he had pushed himself during the final provisioning.

He took one last look at the watch scrambling overhead through the jungle of rigging, spars, and sails before going below for the meeting he had called with his Marines. Although most of the crew were new to the *Huma*, they were a familiar mixture of Lascar sailors, island fishermen and nutbrown villagers terrified of the sea. Jud and Groot had drilled the new men arduously in harbour and Horne believed that, without a storm, they could survive the voyage around Ceylon and up the Coromandel Coast to Madras. The difficulty would be to stop them from scattering upon arrival at Fort St. George. Desertion was a greater problem than recruitment, particularly in the larger Indian settlements where many of the crew had relatives or friends.

Horne's cabin was spartan but adequate for his needs. A trestle table; two rough chairs; a canvas hammock; a brass-bound sea chest packed with clothes and his few other possessions, its flat top serving as a wash-stand. Cases dotted the cabin's deck—provisions provided by the East India Company for a captain's use on the voyage.

The trestle table doubled as Horne's desk; he sat behind it, boots crossed in front of him, facing his five Marines as waves crashed against the pitching hull, the sound blending with the creaking of timbers and the harping of taut rigging.

On the desk before him lay a parchment sheet giving him his formal command of the *Huma* for the voyage to Madras. Beside it lay the canvas envelope in which the document had been enclosed, complete with official wax seals. Signed by Bombay's Governor Spencer, the command threw no light on their destination, but Horne now explained as much as he knew to the men lined up in front of him.

"We are to find a company agent who's gone missing from Fort St. George," he began.

The name "Madras" alerted the men.

Fred Babcock spoke first. "The damned Company's not trying to catch us in a trap, is it, Horne? Sending us back into Fort George?"

"That was my first suspicion," admitted Horne. "Nobody but the Governors knows we were inside the fort last April, and why."

Babcock shook his head. "Send us after one missing man? I don't know, Horne. It smells like a trap."

Horne hated to begin every reunion by barking at Babcock about lack of discipline. His demands on the squadron were few, and critics often accused him of lax control. One of the few things he insisted upon, however, was being addressed respectfully by his men, for disrespect led to insubordination; moreover, they were sailing with a new crew for whom an example must be set.

Appraising Babcock's slouched stance, sloppy clothes, tousled hair and unshaven face, Horne, asked, "How long have you been a Marine, Babcock?"

Babcock pulled at a big red ear. "Hasn't a year passed, Horne, since you took us out of prison and trained us on Bull Island?"

"I obviously didn't do my job."

The lumbering American colonial grinned. "I'm alive, aren't I?"

"My efforts reflect poorly on me if you don't even know how to address an officer, Babcock."

Babcock stuck out his bare chest, snapping a salute. "Aye, aye, sir."

Horne sprang from his chair. "Damn it, Babcock. Nothing's a joke except you."

The American held the ramrod-stiff posture, mocking, "But, sir, I'm a Bombay . . . Buccan*eer*!"

The East India Company's Bombay Marines had no more than six frigates and ten galliots patrolling the Company's trading routes and drawing charts for their merchantmen. The Marines, often slipshod in dress, were looked down upon by the Company's Maritime Service, the men who served aboard the merchantmen, and had been dubbed by them, and the men of the Royal Navy, the "Bombay Buccaneers."

Groot interrupted, "Question, please, *schipper*."

Ignoring the Dutchman's request to speak, Horne was still glaring at Babcock. Was there only one way to teach respect to this man? Had the time come to break the rule about not using the lash?

Groot tried again from the other end of the line. "*Schipper*, what job does the missing man do for the

Company in Madras?" As usual, Groot made an attempt
at showing Horne respect, using the Dutch word for captain. It was Groot, too, who always tried to divert attention from Babcock's mistakes or misdemeanours. On
shore between missions, they shared rooms in Bombay.

"A purchasing agent, Groot," answered Horne and
turned back to Babcock. "The man's name is Fanshaw.
He buys goods for merchants back in England."

Horne looked at the other three men, noticing the
Tamil, Jingee, glancing around the cabin at the work to
be done, planning where to stow supplies, move bulk-
heads, serve meals when Horne was using his one table
as a desk.

Groot asked, "*Schipper*, do they have any suspicion
where the man's gone?"

Horne gestured at the letter. "If so, Governor Spencer
doesn't say."

Kiro saluted, touching the red band knotted around his
shiny black hair. "Captain Horne, sir, if the Company's
called the Marine for assistance, does that not mean they
suspect the man's escaped on a ship?"

Horne nodded his approval at the Japanese. "I agree,
Kiro. If they believed Fanshaw had fled, say, across the
Chingleputt Hills, Governor Pigot could have called on
the troops garrisoned at Madras to pursue him. Not the
Marine."

He looked from Kiro to Jud, to Jingee, to Groot. "Although Governor Spencer doesn't allude to the possibility
in his letter, I believe we must also be prepared to deal
with kidnappers."

"Kidnappers, *schipper*?" Groot kneaded the blue cap
he held in his hands. "Men demanding big rewards from
the Company?"

"Possibly." Horne liked firing the men's imaginations

but he hated suspicions running wild. "I mention the point merely for you to consider."

Jingee stepped forward, touching his white turban. "Captain sahib, might not the man, Fanshaw, already be dead? Had his throat cut? His head sliced from his neck. His heart ripped out. His arms and legs hacked from his body. His . . ."

Horne repressed a grin. Wasn't it like Jingee to suspect murder, and a brutal murder at that? Horne had found Jingee jailed for stabbing to death an English factor.

"True, that's another possibility to consider, Jingee," he agreed. "The man might already be dead."

Rising from his chair, he said, "We'll meet again tomorrow. Between now and then there are other things to think about, such as our new men. Study them. See if there are possible recruits for the Marine."

Stopping in front of Babcock, he said, "I expect better conduct from you on this voyage, Babcock."

Babcock repeated his mock salute. "Aye, aye, sir."

Damn it. Doesn't the man ever stop playing the fool?

A hail cut through the sounds of water sluicing against the ship's hull.

"Ahoy . . . ship . . . ahoy . . . ship . . ."

Horne looked to Jud. "Who's up top?"

"The Ceylonese, sir."

"Join him," ordered Horne. "Check what he sees."

Grabbing his spyglass he dismissed all the men, calling after Babcock, "Don't think I'm forgetting about you." He moved toward the door, ordering, "For the moment, get your arse up on the quarter-deck."

4

Open Boat

Sea spray misting his face, Horne lowered the spyglass and saw with his naked eye that the distant white speck was not sun glittering on silver waves but a ship approaching off the starboard bow.

From aloft, Jud verified, "Full sail, sir."

Horne raised the spyglass; he estimated that the ship's foresail was attached to a long boom but doubted if she was a native craft.

"Sloop, sir," called Jud. "Flying no colours."

Beside Horne on the quarter-deck Babcock asked, "Enemy?"

Horne had forgotten about Babcock's indiscipline, all his concentration on the approaching ship. Her foresail might be attached to gaff mast and boom but she was probably not one of the British sloops-of-war often rigged as a brigantine. She might be a packet boat carrying mail and passengers for Bombay, but if so, why was she bearing down on the *Huma*? The frigate flew no flag. A rendezvous with an unidentified ship would be dangerous in these waters so infested with pirates and privateers.

Deciding to test the sloop's intention, Horne called to the helm, "Two points to starboard."

Spyglass back to his eye, he watched the white sail follow his tack and thought again about pirates. He had first sailed these waters seven years ago under Commodore James, Watson's predecessor in Bombay Castle, serving as a midshipman aboard the flagship, *Protector*. The mission had been to flush out Malagasy pirates along the Malabar Coast, but James had remarked that India's western shores could never be totally rid of robbers who preyed on its busy trading routes.

Did the sloop belong to such a Malagasy chieftain?

"Sails ho!" Jud shouted from his perch. "Two sails on the northern horizon . . . two to the south . . ."

Horne swept his spyglass to the left. To the right. He spotted four white specks flanking the sloop, smaller craft which might possibly be a fishing fleet although it was unlikely they would be so far from the coast.

"Sloop coming up fast, sir," reported Jud.

"How many out there?" asked Babcock.

"One sloop and four coasting vessels?"

"Pattimars?"

Horne could not yet make out whether the small craft were native vessels. If they were, they could be fitted with guns, tipping the odds against the *Huma*'s fire power.

"Hoist colours," he ordered Babcock.

"Aye, aye, sir," answered Babcock in unexpected form.

To Kiro, Horne bellowed, "Clear for action!"

Moments later bare feet hurried across deck to the gun stations, Kiro dashing from crew to crew.

When the distant sloop still failed to raise her flag, Horne was convinced she was not approaching for any

harmless exchange of information, for a peaceful rendezvous.

Aloft, Jud hailed, "Ahoy, sir!"

Horne snapped open his spyglass. The smaller vessels
were widening their arc.

Strangely, though, the sloop continued on course . . .

No. She was tacking . . .

Jud had also spotted the change in the sloop's direction.

"Sloop going about."

The mystery vessel was close enough now for Horne
to study the sleek line of her hull. His fist tightened on
the spyglass as he caught sight of her gun ports; had the
cannon been run out? As he watched he saw an object
pass over the gunwale.

"Boat lowered," reported Jud from his perch.

Boat? Why should the captain be lowering an open
craft at such a moment?

The sloop was staying on the silver crested waves. But
Horne ignored the shifting vessel as he scoured the water
for the boat lowered in the change of course. What was
happening? Did the sloop carry a sick man? Was there
disease aboard? Fever?

The *Huma*'s rails were lined with craning necks as the
sloop receded to the east, leaving the small boat tossing
from crest to crest on the choppy ocean.

As Babcock hurried men to lower a rowing crew to
collect the small boat, Horne studied it through his spyglass, watching it fall and rise on the waves.

A strange object caught his eye. Yes, there was a man
in the open boat. He was lying face-up on the thwarts.
A red stain on his chest told Horne that his throat had
been slit. The carved wooden fist attached to his right
hand proclaimed his identity.

5

The Gage

The only sounds were the slush of lapping water against the *Huma* hove-to in the wind and the scraping of rope on a pulley as Jingee's crew raised the rowing boat from the sea. The other hands crowded the larboard rail, staring at the blood-stained corpse sprawled face-upwards in the small craft.

Babcock was standing beside Horne. "Why would somebody put a dead man to sea?"

"For us to do precisely what we're doing," answered Horne. From the quarter-deck he could not only identify the pirate whom Babcock had fought in Bombay but could also see the blotches of scarlet dotting the man's drenched clothes.

"I don't get your meaning." Babcock's earlier swagger had vanished at the sight of the corpse.

"But you recognise him?" Horne pointed at the corpse, wondering if Babcock was being stupid or merely incapable of grasping the ramifications of such a situation. Admittedly, it was bizarre.

"Hell, yes, I recognise him," Babcock mumbled. "It's the guy from back in town. The man I fought." Pulling nervously on his ear, he added, "But why did his mates have to knife him and put him to sea in that peanut shell? Why tie the wooden mitt on his fist?"

Horne began his interpretation of the situation. "The man didn't finish the fight with you and worse than dishonouring himself, he disgraced his friends. To fight and lose is better than not fighting to the bitter end."

"You stopped us," Babcock reminded Horne.

"I'd do the same again. But that doesn't change these people's customs and superstitions. Don't forget, Babcock, they're Malagasy. Proud and steeped in folklore. When such a man is challenged to fight, he is expected to kill or be killed. A fight is fought to the finish. But yours wasn't. Therefore his friends are taking up where he left off. Now. Here."

"Is that . . . law?"

"More like tradition."

"Hell, Horne. I didn't ask to get involved in no tradition."

"If I remember correctly, Babcock, you told the man you could beat him in a fight. Any way he chose."

"True . . ."

"The man chose an old Indian way of fighting. It was to be a fight to the death. But he was denied both victory and defeat so his friends are finishing it for him. With us."

"A dead body? That's a hat in the ring?" Babcock shook his head. "I don't understand any of it."

"The body's their gage. Their challenge to us." Horne added, "They'll be back to see if we accept it."

Against the hazy coastline the sloop glimmered small and white, waiting, while the four native craft dotted the horizon like pearls loosely strung on black wire.

Babcock glanced over his shoulder. "All five of them are coming after us?"

"They want to make certain they finish the fight this time."

"They'll slaughter us."

"That's what they hope to do."

Pulling his ear, Babcock admitted, "It's my fault. It's me they want."

Kiro emerged from the men crowding the port entry. Scrambling up the ladder, he reported to Horne, "Sir, the body's been stabbed many times."

Jingee followed Kiro. "Captain sahib, the man's throat has been slit like a chicken."

Babcock asked miserably, "Why would they slit his throat and then stab him? Why not just throw him overboard in the boat and be done with it?"

Jingee's dark eyes twinkled as he waited to speak. "Captain sahib?"

Horne nodded permission.

Jingee explained in his precisely-spoken English, "The Malagasy detest cowardice, Captain sahib. I suspect they used the man to absorb any unmanliness aboard their ship."

"Like a scapegoat," Horne said.

"Yes, Captain sahib. Such behaviour is difficult for many Europeans to understand. First, the Malagasies slit the man's throat, then probably knifed him in a ritual killing before setting the body adrift."

Jingee's explanation concurred with Horne's own theory. "They put the body to sea for us to find it and haul it aboard. The corpse is our challenge."

Jingee bowed from the waist, complimenting, "I should not be surprised, Captain sahib, that a man like you understands such things."

"Damned savages," mumbled Babcock.

Horne ordered Jingee, "Have the body sewn in a bag."

"Shall I also say prayers over the body, Captain sahib?" asked Jingee.

Horne waved his hand dismissively. His thoughts were on the *Huma* and the fate of his men, not the reincarnation of a pirate into some higher caste in his next life-cycle.

Sending Kiro and Jingee to dispose of the body as quickly and respectfully as possible, he raised his spyglass to see if his hunch was proving correct.

The sloop was changing tack, he saw, and the native craft spreading in formation, two pattimars widening to the north, the other pair gliding south.

Babcock asked, "The buggers coming back?"

Horne was busily formulating an idea, believing that the pirates were creating what might prove to be a claw to close around the lone frigate.

Hove-to, the furling of the fore topsails had quieted the *Huma*, bringing her into the wind. Starboard to the open sea, she rose and dropped on the choppy water, steadied by the staysails.

Giving orders to loose all sail to the wind, Horne kept checking the pirate flotilla's steady progress towards the *Huma*.

At his side Babcock moved uneasily. "We're going to make a run for it?"

Horne scoured the horizon for further sail as he answered. "If they don't get a fight from us, they'll make trouble for some innocent party later."

Babcock frowned at the raider's flotilla. "We're going to take on all . . . five?"

Horne ignored the question, calling to the helm, "Steady as you go, Groot. Steady."

As the mainsails caught the wind, the *Huma* charged forward, the gust heeling her over, waves bursting across the prow.

The tilting deck, the breeze, the shuddering canvas overhead, reminded Horne that he was where he wanted to be. He momentarily forgot about Babcock beside him, even about the threatening enemy, and reflected that he had been too long on land, too long without a command. In Bombay he became short-tempered, pessimistic; he lived aimlessly from day to day.

Looking at the spread sails, he saw the new crew scurrying like flies across the yards. This was not the first time he had seen such a transformation of farmers and herdsmen into sea hands. It would probably not be the last.

Shortage of manpower was becoming too common. Horne seldom enjoyed a full complement of men to divide into four-hour watches with dog watches. He had learned, too, to do without officers, inventing a makeshift rating to adapt to his crew. But, then, if he truly wanted a tightly run ship, could he not always join the Royal Navy?

A touch on his shoulder brought Horne back to the present.

"Horne, I guess I should say I'm sorry."

Did Babcock's indiscipline truly bother him? Why hadn't he taken drastic steps with him before? Did the lack of manpower make him suffer such laxness?

Babcock went on, "Like I said, this is my making."

"Babcock, there's a time and place for apologies. This is not one of them."

"But—"

Over the crash of the waves, Horne shouted, "At the moment we have a battle to fight, Babcock."

"Aye, aye, Captain," answered Babcock cheekily.

Friendship was the problem, Horne realised. He had become too close to his Marines. How do you tie a friend to a grating and lash him for not addressing you properly?

As the *Huma* set a course straight for the pirate flotilla, Babcock remained near Horne on the quarter-deck.

As a boy, Babcock had never dreamt of going to sea. Born on a farm in America's lush Ohio Valley, he had been raised to work the land, destined to marry the neighbour's golden-haired daughter and become part of the pioneer community hewn from the wilderness. When he was nineteen, he quarrelled with his father and ran away from home, working in blacksmiths' forges and on freight lines, doing any odd job he could find as he made his way eastwards, travelling through Pennsylvania, New York, Connecticut, Massachusetts.

His solid muscle and light-hearted disposition helped him readily find work; in Boston, he was signed aboard a trading ship bound for the Orient. But his size also proved to be a disadvantage. Two weeks out of port, an officer picked an argument with him. Babcock fought to defend himself but it was his bad luck to knock the officer's head against a capstan. When the merchant ship called in Bombay, Babcock was sent ashore in shackles and locked in a cell honey-combed deep beneath Bombay Castle. It was from the subterranean prison that Adam Horne had chosen him to become a candidate for the Bombay Marine. Training with Horne on Bull Island had convinced Babcock that he had at last found a niche for himself in the world.

But belonging to Horne's unit also had its drawbacks. The spells between missions were too long; weeks and months spent ashore. Babcock easily became bored, and when he was bored he drank too much. When he drank, he always got into trouble.

He had been drinking when he had met a group of

leather-faced Asians in a Bombay beer shop. They had argued in pidgin English that all *topiwallahs* should get out of India. He had challenged any of the men to fight him in any manner they chose.

The ocean misted against Babcock's bare chest as he gazed out to sea. He knew that Horne had a right to be angry with him; the knife-and-fist fight had been stupid, had put the *Huma* and all the men aboard in jeopardy.

Babcock also had another problem apart from drinking. An older problem.

Why couldn't he address another man as a superior? He tried hard to remember to call Horne "sir" and "Captain"; but he either forgot or the words stuck in his throat. Why? Didn't he like submitting to authority? Couldn't he admit that another man was better than himself, more superior in some way? Why couldn't he pull his forelock and grovel? Did it have to do with the fight he had had with his father years ago in Ohio? In his dreams he often confused the faces of his father and Horne. In his dreams, he often called Horne "pa."

6

Flotilla

The distance was shortening rapidly between the *Huma* and the five-pointed claw of the enemy flotilla: the four pattimars lagged north and south of the sloop in the lead of the wedged attack.

"Run out starboard guns," Horne shouted to Kiro.

Over the rumble of cannon being manned into firing position, he called to the helm, "Lay to larboard tack."

"Aye, aye, *schipper.*"

As the bowsprit swung on the steel-blue waves, Horne remembered that the crew was new and preparing the first time for battle at sea. Looking aloft, he saw small figures grabbing the braces, swinging like monkeys against the yards; the sails thundered as the *Huma* changed onto her new tack.

Satisfied with their performance, Horne raised the spyglass back to his eye to study the approaching enemy. The sloop still maintained her course towards the *Huma* but the southerly two pattimars were attempting to bear round to enclose him. Good. He had anticipated such an action and was planning how to divide the flotilla.

As the *Huma*'s jib boom swept towards the distant

coastline, he trained the glass back on the sloop, looking for any flutter of flags or pennants, some call-signals being hoisted on the sloop to send the leader's commands to the four native vessels.

A distant pop caught his attention. He held the glass on the sloop, seeing a wisp of blue smoke rise from the gunports. The enemy had fired on the *Huma*. But why so soon? Had the blast been a ranging shot or was the commander over-anxious?

"Wait fire," Horne cautioned Kiro.

A second blue puff rose across the waves.

It was often impossible to know anything about an enemy at sea, particularly an enemy in an unmarked ship. Every little movement or action must be studied for information: guns fired too quickly; an impatient turn of the prow. And as Horne looked for clues to his opponents, he likewise tried to prevent them from understanding him. He changed tactics as soon as his intentions might be recognised.

The sloop's commander must be the leader of the Malagasy fleet, he reasoned. The pirate lord had obviously ordered the dead man to be cast overboard in the boat. If so, what would such a blood-thirsty leader do to prisoners taken alive? Was Horne risking his men to cruel torture? Should he try to make flight while he still had a chance?

On a course to angle between the sloop and two southern pattimars, he tried to gauge their intentions.

"Deck ho," hailed Jud from the main mast.

What the devil? Were more ships joining the flotilla? Horne swung the spyglass in the opposite direction and saw that the northerly two ships were also changing course.

He had little time to ponder their movement. He had to deal with the enemy nearer to hand.

Satisfied with the *Huma*'s position relative to the pair of southern native vessels, he ordered, "Starboard guns—"

Kiro held his head high, listening for the final order. His gunners' ears were already bound with bandanas to protect their eardrums from the explosion.

"—fire!"

The deck shuddered under the cannons' recoil.

Watching the hit with his naked eye, Horne nodded as the mast of one pattimar collapsed from a strike. The explosion was like a spark in a tinder-box, the wood and sail bursting into instant flame. Why would such an in-flammable ship carry cannon, let alone take part in action? Horne watched black smoke rise as the crew began diving overboard.

Kiro's strike on the second southern vessel had a less dramatic impact but nonetheless the ship's crew were beginning to dive into the lapping waves.

Horne held his glass on the smoke-laden scene to study the evacuation from the southern two pattimars; he could also see men still on board, trying to wave back the de-serters. He had heard of Hindus abandoning leaders los-ing in battle but he had never before seen it. The native seamen were not afraid of drowning. No, honour came first. Honour prepared them for their next reincarnation.

Aboard the *Huma*, Kiro goaded the starboard crew to reload grape on top of roundshot.

Horne seized the moment to begin the second stage of his plan.

Babcock moved alongside him. "Chasing the big one?"

Horne was concentrating on the helm. "Steady as you go," he called to Groot, eyes now trained on the northern pattimars closing their position toward the sloop as the two burning pattimars fell farther away to the south.

Babcock laughed. Pointing to the north, he said, "The

Lord's on your side as usual, Horne. Sending you not a minute too late—or too soon—to meet that sloop and those two other pattimars."

"The Lord or the devil," corrected Horne. The *Huma* was lagging in her change of tack, but her timing would now be near-perfect to confront the remaining three enemy ships.

The two northern pattimars greeted the *Huma* with cannon fire. Their aim struck short of the target, peppering the surrounding sea with ball and grape.

Seeing that the northern pattimars would be closer to the *Huma* than the sloop, Horne was determined to persevere in his offensive to divide them; the sloop's present tack could only work to his advantage.

Wanting Kiro's eyes as well as his ears, he crossed the quarter-deck and shouted, "Kiro, ho!"

Kiro raised his head.

Horne jabbed a finger towards the larboard gundeck, soon to face the northern pattimars as the frigate swung round; the cannons were already run out and gunners waiting for action. At the same moment, he raised his other hand palm upwards to the starboard guns. Hold their fire.

Understanding the command, Kiro raced across to the larboard guns.

When Horne was satisfied with the *Huma*'s new course, he decided it was time to put the chancy plan into action.

He began, "Larboard guns—"

Kiro crouched near the second crew, ready to shout them into action.

Nerves alive, Horne gauged the range to the pattimars to the north, cautiously proceeding. "Prepare to fire and—"

He looked toward the sloop, its jib boom fighting for new bearing.

Satisfied that the *Huma* had the advantage of a few valuable minutes, he chopped down his hand.

"—*fire!*"

A broadside raked both northern pattimars. But at the same moment, the deck trembled beneath Horne's feet. Damn! The sloop had made her stays and, risking another long shot, scored a strike somewhere below the waterline.

It was futile at the moment to worry about unknown damage. Horne concentrated instead on his plans to isolate the two pattimars from their commander.

Looking towards the helm, he saw Groot grinning at him, cap pushed back on his sun-bleached curls, ready for the next command. A nod from Horne was all it took to set the wheel spinning through his hands.

As the *Huma* heeled in the wind, Horne steeled himself to risk being trapped by the enemy ships and to exploit his position.

Aloft in the shrouds, the watch followed the orders Babcock relayed to them; on the gun decks, the crews waited anxiously for Kiro's next command.

Holding Kiro's eye, Horne pointed to both gun decks.

Stern, voice unwavering, he commenced: "Larboard guns—"

"Larboard guns ready, sir—"

Certain he was not firing too soon, Horne proceeded: "Starboard guns—"

"Starboard guns ready, sir—"

Sluicing water, accompanied by the snap of sails, filled the tense moments as the *Huma* hovered between the two pattimars off larboard, the sloop off starboard.

"—*fire!*"

At the command, both sides of the frigate belched flame. A cloud of smoke engulfed the sea's shimmering face; screams of men filled the air, timber splintering in the acrid explosion.

As the wind slowly began dispersing the smoke, Horne was pleased to see flames licking from both pattimars, and men diving into the waves. Retaliation was now impossible from either ship. The smoke drifting over the water told him that they had also scored damage on the sloop.

Aboard the *Huma*, victorious cheers rose from the crew as the gunners pulled the bandanas off their ears and waved them like pennants.

Deaf to the jubilation, Horne's first thought was of any losses aboard ship. What men had been killed or injured in the strikes? What damage had been done to the ship? What about the enemy? Were all their ships incapacitated?

Looking towards the sloop and studying the chaos beneath her ripped sail, he considered the last part of his plan. This was the moment to move into action.

Reassured that the first two pattimars had receded far to the south, he called over the din of cheers and huzzahs, "Seize arms!"

Babcock laughed alongside him. "Go get them, Horne, yes?"

"Prepare men to board ship," Horne shouted more loudly.

Aboard the pirate sloop, a white flag of truce rose from the smoke, fluttering from the damaged mast.

Horne's eyes darted from the flapping white flag to the two burning pattimars. Somewhere beyond were the other two native craft. Revenge from them was unlikely but possible. If not now, perhaps later. His only insurance for peace would be to incapacitate the sloop when the opportunity was at hand.

7

Boarding Party

The flag of truce failed to convince Horne that the Malagasy's surrender was genuine. Suspicious of treachery, he explained the next stage of action to the crew. "We board in three parties. Keep alert for any traps. Defeat will be bitter for those men."

The babble of excitement spread among Kiro's gun crew as Horne cautioned, "I don't want a blood bath. We're going aboard to muzzle the enemy, keep them from pursuit."

"Babcock," he said, "board men from the prow."

Babcock jumped from the quarter-deck with a whoop.

"Kiro, lead your men from midship."

"Both crews, sir?" Kiro gestured to the men crowded on opposite gun decks.

"Both crews," affirmed Horne.

He looked aloft. "You men up top. I'll lead you from the stern."

A cheer rose from the hands sitting with their bare legs wrapped around spars, clinging to canvas.

"Now, arm yourselves," Horne called.

As the men swung from the rigging, the scramble be-

gan on deck for knives, swords and clubs; Kiro's crew
seized the long ropes attached to spiked grappling irons.
The growing fervour worried Horne. Hand-to-hand combat fuelled a man's appetite for blood lust. Was he wrong
to be ordering a boarding party?

Looking astern, he saw the Malagasy crews abandoning both pattimars, crowding into open boats and clinging
to planks serving as makeshift rafts. His first instinct was
to offer assistance but he dismissed it. What Malagasy
would accept succour from an enemy? Certainly not
those proud tribesmen. Especially not from *topiwallahs*
who had caused their loss of self-respect.

A sword in one hand and a dirk tucked into his waistband, Horne clung to the ratlines as the *Huma* drew
closer to the pirate sloop. Seeing preparations to repel
boarders, he realised he had been correct not to believe
their white flag of surrender. But he also saw pandemo-
nium spreading among their men, more figures jumping
feet first into the sea, clawing through the choppy waves
towards the other evacuees.

Did any of those men now realise how senseless this
battle had been? A stupid loss of ships, not to mention a
senseless waste of lives?

As the gap lessened between the two ships, excitement
mounted aboard the *Huma*. Kiro's crew became increasingly anxious for the call to hurl their grappling irons;
Babcock's men stood ready with long planks to bridge
the sloop's rail.

Clear-voiced, Horne reminded them, "Fight to disable
the ship. Not to spill blood."

A silence fell over the crew, the babble giving way to
the sound of lapping waves and creaking timber. For the
final time, Horne looked aboard the sloop to see if the
enemy might succeed in a defensive manoeuvre. Thankfully, they were not returning to their guns, not preparing

to greet the *Huma* with a sudden broadside.

At last the moment came.

"Throw grappling irons."

As the spiked iron stars crossed the gap, a flood of brown men swung from the shrouds; the second crew rushed their plank bridges, pouring over the rail, the sound of clanking steel and the pop of flintlocks filling the air.

Sword in hand, Horne leaped aboard the sloop and was instantly greeted by a dagger's thrust. Dodging to one side, he swung his sword at the attacker, slashing a line of blood across the man's wrist.

Moving amidship, he stopped when he saw a man lunge toward him; he caught the attacker on his dagger and, summoning his strength, hurled the body overboard into the water.

Bent upon finding the leader, he paused to peer through the smoky confusion, searching for some figure of authority. Certainly the captain had not already abandoned ship.

Turning towards the stern, Horne faced a wild-eyed giant who rushed at him with a scimitar. Jumping aside, he pulled back his own sword but, at the same moment, he caught sight of another man raising a club high in the air. That was the last he remembered.

Kiro took his crew across amidships with a blood-curdling cry. In the prow, Babcock's men already waged battle as Horne led the stern attack.

Kiro had learned the Japanese fighting art of *Karate* in his homeland. Chopping down his hand, he sent a pistol flying. A kick disabled a swordsmen. Quick fingers blinded two more attackers.

Kiro and Horne made a good fighting team, Kiro using *Karate*, Horne practising the ancient Greek technique of fighting, *Pankration*, which he had learnt from an old soldier in England.

Before becoming a Bombay Marine, Kiro had known nothing about Adam Horne or the East India Company. Having been a gunner aboard an island raiding boat out of Nagasaki, he had been captured by a Company merchantman and gaoled for piracy in Bombay Castle.

The rootless day-to-day existence of a Bombay Marine was little different from the life of a pirate—homeless; no family; a life of feast or famine. Constant danger, too, taught a Marine to depend on his physical strength and quick wits. But Horne also instilled a sense of honour into his men. There must be no senseless killings, no plundering, no savage attacks on the defenceless.

Horne showed each man, too, how to get the most out of himself; to evaluate his mental as well as his physical capabilities; to plumb hidden talents; to exercise brain as well as brawn.

On their last assignment, two of Horne's seven Marines had been killed by cannon fire. Kiro had realised that missions ashore were as deadly as sea fighting. There were now only five Marines left; who would be killed next?

Kiro had learnt not to let worry eat away at him. He had no wife, no children, no known ancestors. The only time in his life when he remembered ever being truly frightened was on Bull Island during his training with Horne. He still recalled how his stomach had knotted with nerves when he feared that Horne was eliminating him from the final choices for his Marine unit.

Now, bamboo pole in hand, he rushed a ragged Malagasy, then spun halfway across deck, clipping two other men with either end of the pole, his foot surprising a fourth on the chin.

Righting himself, his eye fell on Horne. A man was attacking him with a cudgel.

Diving for the attacker, Kiro saw in a flash that the man was Chinese, that Horne had been caught unprepared, and that the attack could easily be fatal.

For the first time Kiro thought: What would happen to the Bombay Marines if Horne himself was killed?

8

Ill-Health

"Captain sahib," a voice pleaded in the hazy distance. "You must eat, Captain sahib."

Horne emerged from unconsciousness, aware that he was lying on a narrow bunk, that the bunk was aboard a ship rising and dipping on ocean swells, and that there were figures gathered round him in the ship's cabin, staring at him.

Attempting to raise himself on his elbows, he felt pain stab across his skull and collapsed back onto the thin pallet.

"Captain sahib," implored the voice alongside him. "You must not move, Captain sahib."

The speaker was Jingee; he was dressed in a fresh white cotton tunic and turban, holding a tray with a steaming mug of tea and a plate piled high with golden *chapatis*. Kiro and Groot hovered beside Jingee, their faces set with concern, Groot nervously twisting his blue cap.

Horne tried to speak but, feeling a sickly dryness in his mouth, swallowed and tried again. "What . . . happened?"

"You've been asleep for almost a day, Captain sahib."

"A day?" Horne again tried to raise himself.

Setting down the tray, Jingee hurriedly arranged the hemp pillows behind Horne's head as Groot asked, "Do you remember being struck, *schipper*? Do you remember the boarding party?"

Horne recalled the Malagasy flotilla, the sea battle with the pattimars and sloop, his orders for hand-to-hand combat.

Jingee reminded him, "A few minutes after we boarded the sloop, Captain sahib, someone hit you on the head."

"From behind, *schipper*," added Groot.

Kiro stepped closer to the bed. "But I got your attacker, sir." He cut down the edge of one hand and grinned.

Horne looked in turn at Kiro, Groot and Jingee. "Was anybody killed?"

"None of our men, *schipper*," Groot answered proudly.

"Where's the sloop?"

Holding his blue cap in front of him, Groot replied, "It burned, *schipper*."

"The Malagasies set it afire," elaborated Jingee. "They burn their ships rather than allow them to be captured, Captain sahib."

"The pattimars burned, too?" Horne asked.

"Aye, *schipper*. But their men escaped on rafts and small boats. Probably picked up by the first two pattimars."

"Did we take any prisoners?"

"None, *schipper*."

Jingee interjected with disdain, "The stupid *sudras* prefer to drown than to come aboard a *feringhi* boat."

Horne forced himself to sit higher on the pallet. "Groot, get me details of damages to the ship."

Jingee rushed to Horne's side. "Captain sahib, you must rest."

Horne ignored the throbbing pain inside his head and pushed away Jingee's hand. "Who's in charge of the watch?" he asked. "Who's charting our course?"

"Jud and I chart our course, *schipper*."

Throwing back the coverlet, Horne realised he was naked. "Jingee, bring me my breeches," he ordered.

As Jingee reluctantly handed Horne his clothes, Kiro and Groot answered his questions about crew, the damages the *Huma* had suffered in battle, the repairs done on hull and sails.

Horne only called an end to the meeting when a wave of nausea engulfed him. Reassuring the anxious men that he only needed sleep, he sent them from the cabin and tried to ignore the niggling fear that his injuries were more serious than he was willing to admit.

The *Huma* continued her passage down the west coast of India without further incident. Dirk Groot charted the course through the Gulf of Mannar, taking advantage of the Magercoil winds to pass through the Ceylon Strait and begin the voyage north towards the settlements of Cuddalore and Pondicherry, with hopes of reaching Madras no later than the second week out of Bombay.

Halfway up the Coromandel Coast, Jud spotted the sails of a merchantman flying the red, white and blue pennant of the East India Company. Apart from a few fishing vessels off the south Arcot district, no other ships were sighted.

The sky remained cloudless day and night; the wind decreased after rounding the mainland's tip and the sun's torrid temperature became more apparent as the breeze waned.

Babcock and Jud served with Groot as ship masters,

dividing the watches between them and, in their spare time, selecting men from the crew who showed interest in navigation. At the same time, Kiro drilled new gun crews as well as overseeing the repairs on the ship.

For some days Horne remained too ill to resume his usual place on the quarter-deck. Despite his persistent bouts of dizziness, however, he insisted on spending at least short periods in the fresh air.

His favourite time became the night when the sky was a vast bowl of twinkling pinpoints, occasionally slashed by falling stars. Jud's soft midnight songs drifted over the continuously rolling waves.

Left alone during his nightly vigils, Horne remembered his early days of training on the tumbledown Wiltshire estate of the old soldier, Elihu Cornhill. Cornhill had seen service in Canada and afterwards tutored young students in tactics he had observed among the North American Indians—surprise attack, survival in the wilderness, camouflage. He preferred choosing young men who had been involved with crime, either as a perpetrator or victim. A radical in his thinking, he equated warfare with crime.

As Horne recuperated in his late-night watches, he wondered if there had been a serious gap in Cornhill's training. The old soldier had tutored his pupils for captivity—how to survive solitary confinement, how to resist enemy interrogation; but what does a fighting man do when he is sick or dying? How does a man combat the feeling of sheer uselessness?

Groot diverted his anxiety about Horne's physical well-being into concern about Babcock. There was a delicate subject that he must broach with him.

A light sleeper, since leaving Bombay Groot had been awakened every night in his hammock by Babcock calling out in his sleep, "Pa . . . don't hit me, Pa . . ."

Should he ask Babcock if something was troubling him about his father? Groot spent each forenoon watch at the helm, worrying about his predicament as the gentle slopes and curves of the Coromandel Coast slipped by off the larboard bow.

Groot did not know whether Babcock's father was alive. The five Marines were good friends but no one except Jingee ever talked much about family. The main reason was that most of the Marines had no home ties.

Groot's parents had died in Holland from fever when he had been a small child. As he was shunted from relative to relative, he struggled to keep a cheery face and learned how to entertain himself by escaping into fantasy games. A Viking king, the Sultan of Constantinople, an explorer crossing the Americas—the young Groot had been all by turns, and his dreams for adventure had brought him to India on a Dutch merchant ship before his eighteenth birthday; carelessness landed him in gaol a little over a year later.

Knowing where he could steal a wagon of precious Saidabad silk belonging to the Honourable East India Company, he had made arrangements to sell it and return home to Amsterdam with the money, imagining himself entertaining all his friends and relatives with sumptuous feasts every night of the week.

Unluckily for Groot, the man who had said he was a Dutch trader interested in buying the contraband silk turned out to be an agent for the Honourable East India Company. Groot was sentenced to twenty years in the cells beneath Bombay Castle.

In the two-and-a-half-years which Groot had served of his sentence, he had returned to his fantasy life, planning adventures, imagining himself as everything from an oriental potentate to a gladiator in Rome's ancient games. Since being released from prison by Adam Horne and training to become a Bombay Marine, however, he had found less and less need to day-dream about a life of adventure. Belonging to Horne's elite squadron, he had helped kidnap the French Commander-in-Chief in India, fought pirates in the Indian Ocean, stolen a fortune in gold coins.

Groot's optimistic nature helped him through the dull days ashore between assignments, but recently he was finding it increasingly difficult to share rooms with Babcock in Bombay.

On the last mission, Babcock had bought a monkey in Madagascar. After the animal had almost caused their ship to founder on hidden reefs, Groot had thought Babcock would get rid of the pesky creature. But Babcock had taken the monkey back to the rooms in Bombay, and every night the wretched little beast would wake Groot from his sleep. Nevertheless, Groot tried to control his temper, for he knew Babcock loved the monkey; it was no secret that he would hate to part with it.

Thinking he would be able to sleep peacefully once he was back at sea, Groot found that it was Babcock himself who now disturbed his rest, calling out for his "Pa" in troubled nightmares.

How long-suffering did a friend have to be? Should he tell Babcock about his cries? For some reason he thought the American might be embarrassed by the disclosure. Perhaps he should swap hammocks with Jud or Kiro and let one of them have the problem of telling Babcock.

Groot remembered his Aunt Sophie criticising him many years ago—*You're too considerate for your own good, child. You let your friends walk over you.*

"The encounter with the Malagasies was brief. Damage to the *Huma* insufficient to slow progress . . ."

Horne lowered his pen. Less than a day remained before entering the Madras Roads. He was completing the dreaded task of writing the report for Governor Pigot on the voyage from Bombay to Madras.

The combination of sleep, Jingee's good cooking, and fresh air had rallied Horne's strength. The only thing that troubled him at the moment was a question which Kiro had recently put to him.

"Captain, sir, I have a morbid question to ask," Kiro had announced the previous night on the first watch.

Horne had replied, "I've always been accused of being a trifle too morbid, Kiro."

"What would happen to your Marines, sir, if you were killed in battle."

"The unit as you know it, Kiro, would most likely be disbanded."

Now Horne sat at his desk and wondered if he could leave a squadron in a last will and testament: *To so-and-so I bequeath five men good and true.*

Hmmm. He must consider the idea.

9

Governor Pigot

Governor Pigot rose from behind the gilded desk in his chambers in the Governor's House and extended a small pink hand towards the chair facing him. "Welcome to Fort St. George, Captain Horne," he said.

"Thank you, Your Excellency." Horne was as greatly surprised by Pigot's cordiality as he had been by the prompt summons to his headquarters. The *Huma* had only dropped anchor yesterday in the Madras Roads.

Pigot plopped down in his chair. "I read your report, Captain Horne, and was particularly intrigued with the account of the Malagasy attack. But you didn't mention the taking of any prizes from the infidels."

"The Malagasies burned their vessels to prevent us taking them, Your Excellency."

"You recorded a personal injury, Captain Horne. How serious was it? Do you still suffer? Are there serious complications?"

"I received a slight concussion while boarding the enemy sloop, Your Excellency." Horne regretted having had to mention the incident in the written statement. "I feel greatly improved, sir," he added truthfully.

"Capital. I should hate any incapacity to delay the search for George Fanshaw."

Pigot dropped his eyes to the desk, idly shuffling papers as he added, "Fanshaw's defection took us all by surprise, Horne. But, then, betrayals are always difficult to accept, aren't they?" He looked up at Horne. "Commodore Watson did mention George Fanshaw to you, Horne? The reason I sent for the Bombay Marine?"

"Commodore Watson informed me, Your Excellency, that an agent's missing from Fort St George," answered Horne, noticing that Pigot's manner had become agitated. "Commodore Watson also said, sir, that you would supply me with more complete details."

Pigot pushed his chair back from the desk and folded both hands across the line of pearl buttons fronting his buttercup-yellow waistcoat.

There was a moment of silence in the tall-ceilinged room. Sounds drifted in through the double windows— the footfalls of soldiers marching on cobblestones, the creak of wagon wheels moving towards the native quarter, the distant crash of the surf beyond the fortress's eastern sea wall.

"You're familiar enough with Company hierarchy, Horne," Pigot began more composedly, "to know that a senior merchant is responsible directly to the Governor. This is true in all three presidencies—Bombay, Calcutta, and here in Madras."

As Horne listened, he decided that, despite Pigot's reputation for being an obstinate and sullen man, he had a definite congeniality to him. Or perhaps it was the uneasiness in his voice which mellowed him.

Pigot proceeded, his anxiety becoming plainer. "Watson should have told you, too, that gold's missing from our coffers, Captain. But the missing gold's not the worst part."

What could be more important to the East India Company than gold? Horne could not imagine. It was no small wonder that Pigot was vexed.

His florid face quivering with frustration, Pigot explained, "Damned Fanshaw also took the *China Flyer.*"

The name meant nothing to Horne.

"Raising a crew from the dregs of the Black Town, Fanshaw seized the *China Flyer* and set off across the Bay of Bengal. We know for certain he's gone as far as the Strait of Malacca because one of our Indiamen sighted the *China Flyer* off the Nicobars. The frigate's graceful as a sylph. She was flying no colours but she's easily recognisable. Plies between Madras and Canton on a regular trading course."

Pigot jumped up from his chair. Clasping both hands behind his frock-coat, he started pacing the floor. "A damned clever man, Fanshaw is. Audacious as hell. And clever. Clever as a hungry monkey."

He waved one hand at a nearby window, explaining, "The surf here's a large part of the problem. The Madras Roads are notorious. No harbour. No piers. Nothing but those damned rushing breakers. Makes landings bloody difficult. To-ing and fro-ing in those native craft gives the best of sailors quite a soaking."

Horne pictured the awkward native boats, the *masulahs*, which carried travellers back and forth between anchorage and shore; deep, pliable boats manned by a single oarsman and frequently capsizing.

"But weighing anchor," Pigot continued. "Getting the hell out of here. Ah, now. That's a different matter. Quick pursuit is nigh on impossible."

He wagged a stubby finger at Horne. "George Fanshaw's no fool to take advantage of the Madras Roads. He boarded the *China Flyer* and weighed anchor before his absence was missed."

He resumed his nervous pacing. "But Fanshaw's also a greedy man and that will ultimately be his undoing. You see, Horne, George Fanshaw undoubtedly plans to take advantage of his participation in Company business to profit from the China trade. I know that well enough to stake my life on it."

"Excuse me, Your Excellency," Horne cautiously interrupted. "But you say China? Is that where Fanshaw's gone?"

"China? Of course. What's beyond the Malay peninsula but the South China Sea? What's there apart from . . . China?"

"So he chose to sail there on the—" Horne paused for the name. "—the *China Flyer*."

"A ship familiar to the Hoppo in Macao. You understand, Fanshaw must receive permission at Macao—a 'chop,' they call it—to progress up the Pearl River to Whampoa and Canton . . ."

Pigot paused to study Horne, asking as if it were an afterthought, "What do you know about China, Captain Horne? The island of Macao? The traders of Canton? The Hoppo?"

"Only what I know through study and hearsay, Your Excellency."

Pigot nodded. "Let me explain a little of what awaits you in China, Captain Horne."

Governor Pigot anxiously paced the red-tiled floor of his chambers, hands clasped behind his frock-coat as he gave Horne a brief lesson in the history of the Honourable East India Company and China.

"England's trade with China goes back further than our ties with India. One century and a half. As you know, Captain, the Company is now firmly entrenched here in

India. But, after a hundred and fifty years, we've scarcely tapped the riches of China. Why?"

Pigot paused behind Horne's chair, answering his own question. "The Chinese are an obstinate people, Captain Horne. They refuse to bow to foreigners, whereas we ourselves have to kowtow—literally bang our foreheads on the decks of our ships—in front of them and pay dearly for every scrap of silk we get our hands on."

Horne was pleased that Pigot could not see the smile on his face.

Walking on, Pigot elaborated. "I believe the year was 1612 when we opened a post at Firando. That's in Japan. It was from Firando that the Company expanded to Tai-wan—on the island of Formosa—and to Amoy, a port on the China mainland. The Ming Dynasty ruled China then and were relatively favourable to foreign merchants putting down roots there.

"Spurred on by a modest success, the Company de-cided to expand to Canton. But there we came squarely up against opposition from the Portuguese. Having es-tablished themselves in China around 1550, they natu-rally resisted our arrival in Macao. But through intercession with the Portuguese governor and—" Pigot smiled. "—and through the use of a little local force, the Company successfully gained a foothold."

Horne was not surprised to hear that warfare had gone hand in hand with the East India Company's trade in China. Cannonfire had also increased their profits here in India.

Pigot lingered in front of a window, staring out at the crashing surf. The narrative seemed to be tempering the agitation he had previously shown. "By the year 1670, the Company had trading houses in both Canton and Ma-cao. But, by then, too, the Manchu had toppled the Ming Dynasty, which created new problems for foreign traders.

"The Manchu see all Europeans as barbarians, Captain Horne. They burned our original ports in Amoy and Taiwan. They only allowed us to continue trading in Canton under very difficult, very costly circumstances. Their demand for gifts is outrageous. The forms and warrants they require are not only time-consuming but frequently without purpose."

Horne held his silence but thought how refreshing it was to hear the East India Company complain about other powers obliging them to toe the line.

Pigot continued from his position by the window. "Each subsequent year, the Manchu's demands grow more burdensome. They appointed an Imperial Superintendent of Custom, the Hoppo, who boards each arriving ship to collect his *cumshaw*—a gift whose value dictates how thoroughly a ship will be searched. Oh, make no mistake about it, Captain. Despite China's profusion of dialects and tongues, they manage to find a common language with our captains, and haggle like fishwives over fees and charges. When they finally agree on a fee, the Hoppo presents a ship with its chop to proceed to Whampoa. That's the port of Canton, as you may or may not know.

"Around the turn of the century, the Manchu appointed an Imperial merchant to work alongside the Hoppo and supervise all foreign trade. From that time, the Hoppo, the new Imperial merchant, and the men of his new agency all had to be plied with gifts. Free trade as we knew it came to an end."

Free trade? Horne bit back a retort. He had heard another version of the story. The Honourable East India Company had insisted on a monopoly with China, appointing an official in China called the *Tai-pan*. It was then that China countered the British request by creating their "Imperial merchant." According to Horne's information, it was the British who originally stopped the free trade with China. The Chinese merely went one better!

Pigot proceeded with his history.

"The Company believed affairs could not become worse but, in 1720, the Manchu introduced a new monster. The Co-Hung. This is a committee of merchants with whom we now have to deal, men called 'mandarins.' The only good thing to come out of this change is that the Manchu now grant European ships permission to stay in Macao for the winter months."

Pigot looked over his shoulder at Horne, saying as an aside, "The advantageous time to sail to China is between Spring and September. A captain must leave with the north-east monsoon which begins in the spring."

Questions were beginning to form in Horne's mind— about China, George Fanshaw, and the ship which Fanshaw had supposedly commandeered from the Madras Roads.

Pigot gripped the lapels of his frock-coat, saying, "Ten years passed before we got our next shock.

"Until 1755, the Co-Hung was not involved in the disposal of foreign cargo. But the Manchu suddenly forbade all trade with small merchants, whether buying or selling, especially those with anchorages outside the harbours. All foreigners must now go directly to Canton and deal with the government-sponsored trade. Naturally this is a ruling made by the mandarins and we can only deduce from it that their powers are on the increase."

Horne asked, "Mr. Fanshaw's familiar with these committees? The Co-Hung? The Hoppo? The mandarins and the gift-giving?"

Pigot paused beside his desk. "George Fanshaw originally came out from London as a clerk. A bright young lad, he learned several Hindu dialects. Then he began learning Malayan. Next Chinese. More and more dialects. He became an important translator for our traders, gradually becoming a trader and agent himself. If there's anything to know about China, Fanshaw knows it."

"And you think, sir, he's in Canton now?"

Pigot's earlier agitation had returned. "Most definitely. He's gone there to buy goods cheap and reap a quick profit back in England. I shall give you more details about Fanshaw after you have studied the charts of Macao, Canton, and the whole area."

Horne thought of the vast South China Sea, and the slim chance of finding one ship in it.

Pigot saw his furrowed brow. "The slightest lead will help the Company, Captain Horne. My suggestion is to make straight away for Macao."

"Shall I have access to the Company's trading records with the Chinese, as well as sailing charts, Your Excellency?" The prospect of embarking soon for China excited Horne, despite the awesome task ahead of him.

"Everything you need to see is in our library, Captain. It's located next to the new arsenal . . . where the old one used to be."

Pigot moved behind his desk. "I dare say, Horne, you know where the old arsenal was." He sat down laughing.

Horne gave a start. It was the first reference that Pigot had made to the Bombay Marine's previous visit to Fort St. George. Horne had ordered the arsenal to be exploded.

Reaching for a sheet of paper, Pigot went on, "I have a letter here for you, Horne, which will serve as permission to use the library."

A few hours later Horne began working his way through the leatherbound chart cases which the secretary brought to his desk in the library. It was not until he had searched through the third case that Horne realised that the charts he was looking for were missing from each set.

Someone had anticipated his visit to the library.

10

The Black Town

Daylight was fading as Horne emerged from the East India Company's library in Fort St. George. Stepping out into Portuguese Square, he glanced over his shoulder at the Governor's House and wondered if he should attempt to see Pigot at this late hour and report that the visit to the library had been fruitless.

He felt certain that it was no accident that he had been unable to find the charts he had hoped to inspect. George Fanshaw had lifted them before he had left Madras. Also, the trade documents which Governor Pigot had authorised him to inspect were totally inadequate. Horne had wanted to study receipts, tax permits, duty permissions. He had hoped to glean names of officials in China he might interview. Pigot had only set aside useless bills of lading, quartering tallies and roll musters.

The hour was late; too late to confront Pigot. As he adjusted his hat over his forehead, Horne decided that he would instead keep his appointment with Groot and Jingee in the native quarter. Perhaps they had had some luck this afternoon in learning about the missing Englishman and the commandeered frigate, the *China Flyer*.

•   •   •

The Governor's House dominated the centre of Fort St.
George, and four stone bastions stood at each corner of
the walled fortress. The widest, longest thoroughfare inside the walls led north from the Governor's House to
the Main Gate. Beyond the North Wall lay the native
quarter, the area of Madras dubbed the "Black Town" by
the British.

Horne moved north from the Governor's House towards the North Wall, passing a double row of neat white
houses lining both sides of Main Gate Street, one side
illuminated by coconut oil lamps.

Activity was livelier on the cobbled street than it had
been earlier this afternoon. Men walked in groups up and
down the thoroughfare. They were mostly British, a mixture of His Majesty's troops and Company clerks. A few
men escorted women dressed in white cottons and wide-
brimmed hats, their parasols rolled up for the day.

The sight of men promenading with wives and sweet-
hearts gave Horne a sudden jab of jealousy. Remembering Isabel Springer, he wondered for the hundredth time
if she would have come out to India to share a life with
him here.

He stopped and chided himself. He would not have
come to India at all if Isabel had not been killed, if she
were still alive . . .

He continued walking, forcing himself to concentrate
on matters in hand. Shoulders hunched, he ambled along
the cobbled streets, wondering what his next move should
be regarding George Fanshaw. He had no doubt that Fanshaw had taken or destroyed all vital charts. He was certain, too, that Pigot had purposely not allowed him to
inspect privileged documents. The East India Company
had suffered one defector. Why risk another?

The iron-studded gates stood open at the end of Main

Gate Street; sentries idled inside the guardhouse; evening strollers entered and departed through the gates without question.

Passing under the North Wall arch, Horne saw that the traders' bazaar was closed for the night. The wooden stalls were stripped of merchandise, except for a few wagons festooned with lanterns—vendors selling hot curries and colourful sweetmeats.

Outside the fortress walls, Main Gate Street continued into the Black Town but paving no longer covered the road. Instead of freshly painted buildings, Horne passed clay hovels, lop-sided pagodas, rows of rickety wooden buildings. A cacophony of bells, pipes, drums and merry laughter sounded all around him; the sweet smell of incense and exotic spices mingled with the stench of smoking charcoal and burning cow dung.

Continuing deeper into Black Town, Horne decided that if the East India Company would not give him the information he needed about China, he should not worry about running to earth the man they were sending him to find. Why should he be so deucedly conscientious when his superiors kept vital information from him?

"*Sahib*, sir?" whispered a man from the shadows. "You alone tonight, *sahib*?"

Horne slowed down and glanced at the man. He looked down the alleyway stretching behind him. Its slanting houses must be the homes of the infamous nautch girls of Madras. Horne remembered the lucky devils he had seen only a few minutes ago promenading with wives and lady friends. He envied those red-blooded men who did not have to contemplate visiting a nautch girl for companionship.

Banishing the pangs of jealousy once more, he continued down Main Gate Street, struggling to keep his thoughts on his duty.

Should he find out if Fanshaw had a wife in Madras? A sweetheart? Cronies in whom he might have confided about China? What had Jingee and Groot learnt about Fanshaw and his friends?

Earlier that afternoon, Horne had met Groot and Jingee in the Black Town for a meal. He had told them about the meeting he had just come from with Governor Pigot. They had agreed to meet later after Horne had visited the Company library; they, meanwhile, would try to sleuth out a few details about Fanshaw and the *China Flyer*.

"Captain," whispered another voice from a doorway. "You like a very good surprise this evening, Captain *sahib*?"

"Captain"? Horne remembered he was still wearing his uniform. How conspicuous he must look in this crowd. He stepped closer into the shadows. Spotting the swinging sign he had been looking for, he removed his hat and ducked his head to miss the low beam as he stepped down from the street to the doorway.

Colonials of every nationality frequently attempted to reproduce aspects of their homeland in faraway countries. The Watsons had created Rose Cottage in Bombay. Horne had seen English gardens in Goa; the Liverpool Card Parlours in Surat; the Manchester Dog Pit in Hyderabad. But the London Tavern in the Black Town was the closest thing to an English alehouse he had ever seen outside England.

Low ceilings. Pegged floor strewn with sawdust. Even British tavern smells which permeated the depth of one's soul. Everything about the London Tavern seemed authentic. The one clue that this was India and not England was that turbans dotted the merry crowd of Company revellers drinking ale from tankards.

Accustoming his eyes to the dim lighting, Horne espied Jingee waving at him from across the room and began picking his way through the drinkers. He had not yet reached the wooden bench by the wall when Jingee began reporting. "I found Fanshaw, Captain sahib. I found somebody who knows where he's gone."

Horne was tired and unable to raise much enthusiasm for Jingee's news.

"Congratulations. You've had more luck than I," he admitted.

"Fanshaw's gone to Whampoa, Captain sahib," Jingee continued. "Exactly as Governor Pigot suspects."

He waited for Horne to take a seat. "I learned from my cousins that an Englishman has been secretly hiring crewmen to sail to . . . Canton!"

Jingee had never before mentioned to Horne that he had relatives in Madras. But there was no place in India where the little Tamil did not seem to have a cousin or an aunt or some distant uncle.

"Was the ship the *China Flyer*?" asked Horne.

Jingee held up the palms of both hands. "I do not know, Captain sahib. The family who gives this news to my cousins is *Vaisya*. Very good caste. Very honourable. But they do not know enough about boats to realise that boats have names like people."

"Is there any way to meet the family—?" Horne began.

He stopped as Jingee raised his hand and beckoned to someone at the door.

Horne turned and saw Groot moving towards the table.

"Sorry I'm late, *schipper*," the Dutchman apologised as he looked around the crowded tavern. "But I made friends with some Austrians and they told me a few things I thought we could use."

Horne ordered ale for the three of them, then he and Jingee gave Groot their undivided attention.

"Lothar Schiller. That's the man who's sailing the *China Flyer*, I think, *schipper*," said Groot, hands folded on the plank table. "Schiller's from Hamburg. He's a soldier-of-fortune but found work recently aboard British ships. A few months ago he got a job he didn't want to talk about to his friends. He would only say he planned going to the South China Sea."

"Is he a big man, this Schiller?" asked Jingee.

"Tall and—" Groot shrugged. "—about as big as Babcock, as far I can understand." The question puzzled him.

"What colour's his hair?" asked Jingee.

"Yellow. Like mine. Why?"

Jingee turned to Horne. "This Schiller man must be the same person my cousins' friends spoke about."

Groot looked inquisitively from Jingee to Horne. "You two know something you're not telling me?"

Jingee hurriedly repeated the story he had heard from his cousins' friends, the family whose son had been hired to sail to China with an Englishman who had told him to keep his destination a secret.

"The family only knew that the captain of the ship on which their son would be sailing spoke German," he said, "and had hair—" He pointed at the tavern's low ceiling. "—bright like the sun."

"It's not much of a clue," said Horne. He held up his tankard, adding, "But it's a start."

The coconut oil lamps of Fort St. George twinkled in the night as Babcock stood aboard the *Huma* in her anchorage in the Madras Roads.

Despite the majestic sight of the turreted fortress stretching along the moonlit shoreline, Babcock was feeling dejected. The sensation was unusual for him, but he knew it was serious because he did not even miss his pet monkey. When Monkey couldn't make him laugh, something was seriously wrong.

Horne no longer reproached Babcock for fighting the

Malagasy pirate in Bombay. Babcock thanked the Lord that nobody had been killed in the sea encounter. He would have blamed himself for any casualties suffered aboard the *Huma*. When would he ever learn to keep his big mouth shut and avoid getting into brawls?

Was that what was bothering him? Fighting with the Malagasy? Being responsible for the poor devil getting his throat slit and being thrown overboard in the open boat?

Perhaps his recent nightmares were at the root of his problem.

For the past fortnight, Babcock had been dreaming about brawling with his father. Halfway through the fist-icuffs, his father would turn into Adam Horne and Babcock would stop fighting, always refusing to strike his Captain. Covering himself with both arms, he would beg Horne not to hit him. But in the dream Babcock called him "Pa" rather than "Horne"— *"Don't hit me, Pa. Don't hit me."*

A sign of cowardice? Was that what those dreams meant? Was he frightened of fighting Horne?

Looking across the crashing Madras surf, Babcock's mind went back to the days when Horne had first brought his Marines to Fort St. George. Babcock had travelled overland with Bapu, Mustafa and Groot in a dung cart. Bapu, an Indian, had subsequently been killed at sea— the first of Horne's Marines to die. The next casualty had been Mustafa the Turk.

Only Groot and Babcock himself were left from that overland party. Babcock turned his back on the fortress. Leaning against the railing, he looked at the stars twinkling in the east and wondered where Horne would next take his Marines. Which one of them, this time, would not return to Bombay?

PART TWO
The Pursuit

11

Lothar Schiller

The winds off the Philippines raised waves around the *China Flyer*, tossing the deck and yawing the masts in wild circles. A storm must be brewing, Lothar Schiller predicted. But, worse, he worried about the anger growing inside him at the Englishman, George Fanshaw.

"Reduce sail," he ordered his Indonesian lieutenant, Looi. "Topsail and spanker—double reefs."

In these waters of the South China Sea a wind could fall as quickly as it rose, but Schiller decided not to take a gamble. The precaution of having the sails clewed and furled also gave him time to cool his temper. He did not want to spend another day quarrelling with Fanshaw. In the two months since they had left Madras, it seemed they had done nothing but argue. The disagreements had begun a few days out of Madras when Fanshaw had ordered Schiller to divert from the course to Canton. Determined to find opium to present as a *cumshaw* in Canton, he had directed Schiller on a meandering course around Borneo, through the Sulu Sea, north to the Philippines and back to the south, risking attack from Sulu pirates. After six weeks of search, they had located a storehouse of opium on the Sulu island of Cherang. Fanshaw had persuaded the natives to sell but, when the last chest had been stowed aboard the frigate, he had ordered Schiller's men to fire on the village.

Hearing footsteps behind him on the quarterdeck, Schiller turned and saw Fanshaw approaching him.

Speak of the devil, he told himself.

"A storm brewing?" asked Fanshaw, face upturned to the clear blue sky. "Or merely a lively gust to help us on the last leg of our journey to Canton?"

"Better be prepared for trouble than sorry," answered Schiller in his heavily-accented English.

"Safe, perhaps. But—" Fanshaw kept his back to Schiller as he studied the nut-brown hands swinging from the masts. "—will not orders to furl sails also slow us down in reaching Macao, Mr. Schiller?"

"We go even more slow, Mr. Fanshaw, if we lose all our masts in a storm." Schiller's accent became thicker as anger boiled inside him. If the Englishman did not approve of the way the ship was being sailed, why did he not come right out and say so? Why did he hint and talk in circles, always making sly criticisms?

"We cannot afford to lose time, Mr. Schiller," reprimanded Fanshaw, "merely because you suspect a storm. We spent more time sailing through the Sulus than I had intended. We've already been two months at sea."

"I do only what I think best for the ship, Herr Fanshaw."

"You would also do well to concentrate on getting us to Canton as quickly as possible."

Schiller brought up a subject he had raised time and time before. "The voyage might go faster, sir, if you let me study all the charts. Not just bits and pieces. One chart today. One chart tomorrow. One chart the next day."

"I don't see how that could speed our passage, Mr. Schiller."

"Sir, you've made this passage up the South China Sea many times, but this is my first venture here. If I could study the islands ahead of us, sir, I might organise the men for sailing; faster time, the right currents. You see, *ja*?"

"You have got us this far, Mr. Schiller, have you not?"

What the hell! Schiller decided to speak his mind.

"Why do I feel, Mr. Fanshaw, you do not trust me? You don't even pay me a penny yet. You promised me a fortune if I sailed this ship for you. But you still don't give me a penny. I cannot even pay the men a little something."

"Pay the men? Good heavens, Mr. Schiller! Where are these men going to spend money?"

"Men work better with a few coppers in their hands, Mr. Fanshaw."

Fanshaw's voice hardened, his diction becoming more clipped. "Your men can go back to the gutters of the Black Town where you found them, Mr. Schiller, if they don't like my arrangements."

Schiller bristled at the remark, forgetting discretion in his resentment.

"Last week, Mr. Fanshaw, you promised to pay the men if they fired on that village."

"You mean when *you* refused to obey my instructions to order them to fire, Mr. Schiller?"

"But the villagers had given us water and food. You got your cargo there. Why should I order their village to be destroyed?"

"I intend to give the Sulu opium to the Co-Hung as a gift. But I have no intention of letting the Sulus tell everybody who comes along that I've been there."

"So you fire on them? Is that how you repay generosity

and friendship?" Schiller shook his head disbelievingly. "Who were they going to tell? Who is going to know you've been there?"

Slyly, Fanshaw answered, "Have you not thought, Mr. Schiller, that the East India Company might send somebody after us? Have you not heard of the Bombay Marine?"

"For that you destroy a village? Murder defenceless people?"

"Your men were quite ready to act, Mr. Schiller, when they found there was money in it for them."

"Blood money," Schiller said. "And you still haven't paid them for that crime. You even fail to pay your . . . blood money, Mr. Fanshaw."

"Mr. Schiller, I refuse to discuss this any further with you. You would be wise to forget the past and concentrate on the future."

"Yes, Mr. Fanshaw. What about the future?" Schiller folded his muscle-knotted arms across his chest. "You and I have still not discussed what happens after we leave China. Where do we sail from Canton? Do we collect cargo there and return to Madras? Have you signed to join a convoy to England? What are your plans?"

"I'll explain everything to you in good time."

"You say one thing, then another, Mr. Fanshaw," Schiller persisted. "You tell me to think about the future and then do not tell me what the future is."

"Everything in good time, Mr. Schiller," Fanshaw repeated smugly. Again, he raised his head, studying the flapping canvas.

Hell! Schiller cursed himself for ever getting mixed up with a cad like Fanshaw. He had inquired about the man in Madras before agreeing to sail him to China. Fanshaw enjoyed a good reputation as a Company merchant but had no personal friends. Schiller's doubts about his integrity had started when Fanshaw had begun demanding complete secrecy over the forthcoming voyage. He had even refused to tell Schiller the name of the ship he would be sailing, or the nature of the voyage, until a fortnight before they were to leave. When Fanshaw had finally confided that he wanted Schiller to commandeer the *China Flyer*, the latter had refused to be part of the venture. Who needed to spend the rest of his life in gaol? His resistance had collapsed, however, when Fanshaw had promised him more gold than he had ever dreamt of. He had co-operated with the criminal plan.

Schiller was as angry with himself as he was with Fanshaw.

Damned lumbering German! George Fanshaw slammed the door of his cabin, furious at Lothar Schiller's badgering questions. Why couldn't an underling take orders and keep his peace?

Fanshaw considered all the members of a ship's crew— from the captain down to the lowest loblolly boy—to be no different from grooms, ostlers, porters or footmen. All were servants in his view.

Fanshaw knew about servants. His family had been in domestic service for five long, abject generations. Only through hard work and dedication to self-improvement had Fanshaw himself been able to climb out of subserviency and carve a niche for himself in, if not the gentry, at least the merchant class.

The transformation had been systematic and of long duration.

First, changing his surname from Fykes, Fanshaw had found employment far away from England, in India. As a clerk for the East India Company, he had developed an educated accent, watched the mannerisms and dress of his social betters, and spent every free minute studying the dialects of the people with whom the Company traded.

Now he moved across the cabin's pitching deck, undoing his stock and peeling off his frock-coat in the stifling heat as he gloated over what was to be the most important step in his climb to a higher class.

At present, the East India Company had a trade monopoly with China. No other British company had ever successfully challenged its exclusive trade with Canton. The families of the Company's founders were now entrenched in England's highest society—as well as enjoying great wealth.

It had occurred to Fanshaw a few years ago that, with ample financing and the correct political connections, some brilliant man—or group of men—could break the Company's grip on trade with the Manchu mandarins. Then, two years ago, on a return visit to England, he had met Benjamin Cowcross, a stockholder in numerous ships sailing to the Orient. Cowcross had expressed casual interest to Fanshaw in making more than his usual seventy-five per cent from his investments with the Company. Private meetings ensued between the two men, Cowcross impressing Fanshaw as a coarse man but somebody with an adventurous business sense; Fanshaw impressing Cowcross with his knowledge of China and the lucrative trade with the Chinese.

Cowcross had listened avidly to Fanshaw's plan for setting up a company to rival the East India Company. But he worried that the plot might be exposed. He did not want to be excluded from investing in further Company ventures. Finally, he had promised Fanshaw that he would make him a partner in a trade syndicate if an oath could be procured from the Manchu government that they would trade with a second British company.

The pitching of the cabin's deck brought Fanshaw's thoughts back to the present.

He gripped the edge of the desk, listening to the screech of the wind as it tore through the rigging.

Damn! That German lout was right. A storm was brewing.

Frustrated at the possibility of losing more time on this voyage, Fanshaw saw that he must persuade Schiller to press ahead, whatever the weather.

Before he left the cabin, however, he paused to put on his frock-coat and stock. A gentleman must always look the part, and never let the underlings see him improperly attired.

12

The Doldrums

Six days south-east of Madras, the *Huma* passed the verdant island of Pulo Penang and moved through the Malacca Strait. Then, west of Borneo, without warning the sea became as smooth as glass, its blue surface unruffled by the slightest breeze. Horne waited for a gust to rise and speed them further into the South China Sea, but the sails hung limp from their yards.

The abrupt disappearance of all wind puzzled the crew. Horne tried to reassure them as they gathered amidships.

"It's not unusual, men, for the breeze to fall near the equator. One extreme follows another. A few days earlier we could have been tossed about by a storm."

A hum passed through the half-naked seamen, the natives of the area confirming Horne's words with nods of agreement.

"We can't sit around waiting for a breeze," Horne said more forcibly. "There's work to do."

Inventing chores to keep the men occupied, he ordered Jud and Groot to lead yard drills. Kiro was set to race gunners back and forth from larboard to starboard stations, Jingee to teach novices how to mend sails. Babcock took a work gang below deck to repack the stores.

During the forenoon watch of the second windless day, Groot and Babcock reported to Horne's cabin. "The men are beginning to feel restless and trapped, *schipper*," Groot announced.

Babcock stabbed a finger at the stern window. "Trapped in the middle of all this bloody salt water and worried about dying of thirst."

"Reassure the men we have ample fresh water supplies," said Horne.

"They ask what do we do, *schipper*, when all our drinking water's gone."

"During both the past two nights, Groot, there's been a heavy downpour. Prepare the first and middle watch to catch rain-water."

"What about shade, *schipper*?" asked Groot. "During the day there's nowhere for the men to get out of the sun."

Horne glanced at some drawings on his desk. "I've been making plans for temporary shelters."

"*Schipper*, the deck's so hot we have to tie coverings on our bare feet."

Babcock chorused, "Below deck it's a bloody oven. I can't work men down there for more than an hour at a stretch."

Horne acted on Groot's and Babcock's report, cutting the watch hours. He also showed the men how to stretch canvas awnings along the ship's railings. The makeshift shelters allowed protection from the sun as well as giving them a spot from which they could fish for the brightly coloured fish swimming unafraid near the water's calm surface.

"But don't get any ideas about jumping overboard to cool off," Horne warned the crew.

"Swim, swim," a Malayan sailor bragged, moving both

brown arms in front of his naked chest, making the swimming gestures of a turtle.

"No," Horne said firmly. "No swimming."

He raised his forefinger and, moving it round and round in a circle, he pointed another finger at the mirror-like sea, warning, "Sharks."

The quarter-deck awning under which Horne had rested during his recovery from the head wound was once more brought out of the hold. Horne gathered his Marines in its shade to listen to the Chinese linguist, Cheng-So Gilbert, whom Governor Pigot had assigned to them as their interpreter in China.

Of Chinese and English extraction, Cheng-So Gilbert was short and pudgy, with tawny skin and shiny black hair hanging down to his narrow shoulders. Seated cross-legged on a red satin cushion, Cheng-So Gilbert explained, "The city of Canton is closed to all foreign visitors. You cannot go beyond the main gates."

"I thought Canton was China's one port open to all foreigners," protested Groot.

"Foreigners are welcome in Whampoa," answered Cheng-So Gilbert, his moon-face set in its habitual half-smile. "Whampoa is the port of Canton. But foreigners cannot go inside the walled city."

"Why?" asked Babcock. "Are the buildings inlaid with diamonds and rubies? Are the streets paved with gold bricks? Are they scared we're going to come along and take a few back home with us?"

Cheng-So Gilbert explained patiently. "Canton is very plain by Oriental standards, mister. Some men even call it ugly. I cannot give you the true reason why outsiders are not welcome there, but I can repeat a reason I once heard:

"Many years ago there was famine in the countryside.

In Canton, many citizens tilled gardens and kept cattle. Hundreds of farmers flooded to the city to find food. That was when the walls were first built: to protect Canton from hungry outsiders."

"We aren't going to steal rice." Babcock pulled his red ear. "We just want to take a look around the place."

"Ancestors make rules to be obeyed," Cheng-So Gilbert answered diplomatically. "But please do not feel you are missing anything by not seeing Canton, mister. As I say, the city is without architectural virtue. It is not a beautiful place. Also, the Cantonese shout at strangers. They are not a hospitable people. Believe me, mister, you would not be happy there."

Kiro spoke up from the other side of the circle. "You'd do well to believe him, Babcock. The Chinese do nothing but shout and scream. But they have so many dialects, even *they* do not know what they are all complaining about."

With an effort, Cheng-So Gilbert gave the Japanese Marine an amicable smile. "It is true, Captain Horne," he said. "There are many dialects in China." Closing his eyes, he clasped his tiny hands together and, bowing his head, confided, "I speak seventy-eight."

Babcock whistled. "That includes English?"

"Of foreign tongues I speak eleven."

Jingee's eyes widened. He prided himself on his knowledge of languages, but his tally was far below the number of tongues spoken by Cheng-So Gilbert.

Ever the diplomat, the Chinaman continued, "But you do not need to understand people's words to know when they do not want you in their city. The citizens of Canton will throw rocks at you. They will set their dogs on you. I have seen it."

"Dogs?" Jud nudged Kiro. "Maybe I'll stay aboard ship when we reach China. I don't like dogs biting me."

Kiro laughed. "How do you like *eating* dogs? The Chinese find them delicious."

Babcock's upper lip curled in disgust. "It's true? Chinese eat dogs?"

Cheng-So Gilbert answered, "Dogs are often served in China, yes, mister. My favourite dish, though, is a waterfowl which you will see in Whampoa's harbour. You can recognise the bird by its warble."

Cheng-So Gilbert closed his eyes and, pursing his red lips, pulled on his Adam's apple to make a long, gurgling sound.

Horne joined in the men's laughter, amused by the interpreter's bird-call.

He brought the subject back to safety. "You say it's safe to walk along the wharves of Whampoa?"

Cheng-So Gilbert nodded. "Yes, yes, Captain Horne. Whampoa is safe. Whampoa is very safe place. The Manchu desire free trade in Whampoa. You will be safe in Whampoa. In Whampoa you will see ships from many foreign countries. France. Denmark. The Netherlands. And, of course, England."

"How far is Canton from Whampoa?" Horne asked.

Cheng-So Gilbert pressed his tiny hands into an arch, dipping his head respectfully as he answered, "The distance between the port of Whampoa and Canton, Captain Horne, is eighteen miles."

The reply pleased Horne. It was the same number listed on the chart.

Next to him, Jingee asked, "Please tell us about the island of Macao, Mr. Gilbert. Is it near the port of Whampoa?"

"Macao is located in the Pearl River estuary. From Macao pilot boats will escort the ship to Whampoa. The trip up the Pearl River will last a full day."

"Pearl River?" asked Babcock.

"The Pearl River flows from Canton down to the sea."

"With the island of Macao at the mouth?" verified Groot.

"That is correct."

"Do the people shout at foreigners in Macao?" Babcock asked.

Jud added, "And set dogs on you?"

"No, no, no. Macao is controlled by the Portuguese. You are safe in Macao."

"Portuguese." Groot frowned. "Papists."

"It is true. The Portuguese have missions on Macao. The Jesuits have made good friends with the Manchu." Folding his hands, Cheng-So Gilbert added proudly, "I had the honour of studying at the feet of those learned men of God in black robes."

Horne made a mental note of the fact that his interpreter had been a student of the Jesuits.

Cheng-So Gilbert continued, "In Macao, you must only be wary of the sampan people. They are full of tricks and will try to sell you everything. When they are not trying to sell you something, they might be trying to steal from you." He laughed. "The sampan people are despised and detested by all good Chinese. They not only move through Macao, picking pockets and stealing laundry, but they move about the coastline in their sampans, behaving like the Sulu pirates behave in their praus."

Questions bombarded the interpreter.

"What are sampan people?"

"Sulu pirates? Who are they?"

"What's a sampan?"

"Tell us about pirates."

Cheng-So Gilbert held up the palms of his tiny hands as if to ward off the barrage of questions. Cheeks round and jolly as he laughed, he answered, "First, let me explain what I mean about the Sulus.

"As you know, mister gentlemen, the Sulus are the most evil, most deadly pirates in all the east. The Sulus sail in the Sulu Sea in their long narrow boats called 'praus.'"

"Sulu Sea?" Groot, horrified, pointed eastward. "You're talking about the sea at the other end of Borneo? On our sailing route?"

Babcock frowned. "We're not sailing anyplace with no wind, cheesehead."

Cheng-So Gilbert turned to Groot. "The Sulu Sea lies to the east of the South China Sea. North of the island of Celebes."

"And there are pirates there?" asked Jud.

Kiro leaned forward. "The Sulus are known pirates around the China Sea."

The other Marines looked at Horne, memories of the Malagasy attack fresh in their minds.

Wanting to keep the subject on China, Horne turned to the interpreter. "You warned us about sampan people, Mr. Gilbert," he said. "Can you expand a little on that subject?"

"Sampans, as you know, are boats. Sampans have small reed cabins in the middle and do not venture out of sight of land. Since the Manchu Dynasty has come into power in my land, more and more people live on sampans than when the Ming emperors sat on the throne. One theory is that more people in China are homeless than before, that they must live on boats because they do not have land to live on."

"Who are these Manchu you keep talking about?" asked Groot. "The new kings of China?"

Cheng-So Gilbert once more digressed to explain how, in the previous century, Manchu invaders from the north had overcome the decadent Ming Dynasty. The Manchu were keen businessmen, he told them; they had devised a plan to control market prices whereby they stored imported goods in sheds on their arrival in China, keeping them under lock-and-key until all foreign ships had docked, thus avoiding fluctuating prices.

Horne did not know how much of this was true, nor how these snippets of Chinese history could be put to use in the search for the *China Flyer*. Nonetheless, he listened with interest, intrigued by Cheng-So Gilbert and his stories.

For some reason, however, he did not wholly trust the roly-poly man. Why?

While Gilbert was explaining the Chinese respect for ancestors, Horne heard a hubbub rise from the bows.

Looking beyond the port beam, he saw a splashing break the smooth surface of the sea, and a swimmer waving back to his friends on deck.

Damn! Who was disobeying his orders by going swimming? Horne jumped to his feet.

The other Marines followed down the ladder, Cheng-So Gilbert lagging behind, his red satin cushion under one arm.

Horne pushed his way through the crew, immediately recognising the man in the water as the Malayan who had bragged about being able to swim.

"You damned fool," Horne bellowed through cupped hands. "Get back here."

Laughing, the man splashed and waved at Horne, calling, "Swim-swim."

Frustrated, Horne looked around him. He could dive into the water and try dragging the man aboard. If he resisted him, he could knock him unconscious, tie a rope round him, and haul him up over the side.

Feeling a tap on his arm, he glanced round.

Beside him, Jingee stood pointing at the sea.

The crew had also seen the fin breaking the water; they

began shouting at their friend, calling him to come back
to the ship.

No sooner had the swimmer turned to look over his
shoulder to see what the others were pointing at than he
disappeared beneath the sea's smooth surface.

Horne felt his stomach sicken as he watched the struggle that broke the sea's calmness, the swimmer's arm
shooting up, then redness colouring the blue. More fins
circled the spot where the swimmer had been.

A silence fell over the *Huma* as the men lined the rail,
staring helplessly down into the water; no sign remained
of their friend—only blood colouring the smooth sea, and
the fins of circling sharks.

13

The Praus

A torpor fell over the *Huma* after the killing of the Malayan swimmer. Horne knew better than to push the men for the remainder of the afternoon in the jobs invented to fill their idle hours. He suggested that Jud read from the Koran for the victim's soul and then allowed the crew to settle under their sun shelters, to fish and exchange stories while they awaited the evening meal. When the supper of rice, fish and dates was finished, and the sinking sun coloured the still water in a lurid spectrum of purple and red, a Hindu began strumming a sitar and singing a dirge.

The musician's haunting voice drifted through the humid night as Horne sat behind the desk in his cabin, staring blankly at the motionless flame glowing on a squat candle. What could he do to raise the men's spirits? There was ample drinking water, no imminent threat of running out of food, but the swimmer's death had exacerbated the general lethargy. Should he organise them into teams to tow the *Huma* across the hammered-steel water in rowing boats? Make them at least think they were doing something to escape their trap?

Then he turned to brooding about the nature of his search for the *China Flyer*.

Governor Pigot had produced charts to replace those which Fanshaw had presumably taken from Fort St. George. He had also assigned Cheng-So Gilbert as a translator to Horne, and given the *Huma* a small cargo of cloth and opium to present as a *cumshaw* to the Chinese officials in Macao and Whampoa. Horne had been granted full licence, too, in the way he chose to bring Fanshaw back to Madras to face criminal charges. Pigot had assured him that the monetary worth of the *China Flyer* would be divided amongst his crew if they brought the ship home as a prize.

Those preparations and precautions were incidental, however, to the search itself. Had Fanshaw reached Canton by now, or would Horne have to scour far-flung islands and follow China's meandering coastline? Pigot had set him no time limit; how long should he continue the search? It might take him years. Meanwhile Fanshaw could easily disappear to another part of the world.

The *Huma*'s danger might be greater if Fanshaw had already arrived in China, for he could well be mustering support from the Chinese in anticipation of pursuit by the Bombay Marine. From what Horne had heard, Fanshaw was not a stupid man, unlikely to steal a ship from the East India Company and undertake such a bold venture without expecting repercussions. Anticipating that the Company would send the Bombay Marine in search of him, he might well be leading them into a dangerous trap.

What did Fanshaw hope to achieve by taking a Company frigate? Horne wondered. Did he think he could steal Company gold without precipitating a hue and cry? Horne could not imagine any man risking a respected position within the Company hierarchy to abscond to a safe haven in China. Pigot might be correct: Fanshaw was going to China to make a fortune. But where would he live thereafter? Did he have highly-placed friends in England to protect him from the law? The East India Company certainly had the power to prosecute him there, and in India.

On the other hand, Horne could understand a man venturing all for a truly audacious plan—such as setting out to establish a rival trading company. He would need rich and influential contacts in England for such an ambition, but they might also be ready to defend his actions against criminal allegations made by the Honourable East India Company. If such a plan proved to be true, Fanshaw would be using all his previous knowledge from the Company to enormous advantage, taking secrets and privileges to the new company like a traitor defecting to another country.

Horne returned to his old complaint. Why didn't the East India Company entrust him with more information, or at least discuss the issues with him? It was always so easy to despatch—and dismiss—a Marine.

The time was shortly after the first hour of the morning watch. Tossing fitfully from worry and the cloying heat, Horne had finally fallen asleep in his bunk.

Hearing a call, he sat bolt upright in the darkness, his nakedness covered with beads of perspiration.

Had the cry come from the mainmast?

Blinking in the dim cabin, he thought: Was I dreaming?

The hail came a second time.

"Sails ho . . . sail to north-east . . ."

Pulling on his breeches and grabbing his spyglass from the rack, Horne bounded from the cabin. As he dashed up the companionway, he realised that if a ship was approaching the *Huma*, then, by God, there must be a wind in the vicinity.

Daylight was bleaching the sky to the east, the early morning blackness fading into white, lavender, grey.

Standing on the quarter-deck, Horne scanned the north-eastern horizon with his naked eye but saw nothing, not even a pattern of ripples on the inky-black waters. Raising the spyglass, he studied the distant haze through the lens, but still he saw nothing.

What had Jud spotted?

Looking up at the mainmast, Horne's eyes lingered on the topgallant. What was that? A flutter to the canvas?

"Sail ho!" hailed Jud. "Sails to north-east!"

Around the deck, men were beginning to stir in their hammocks, word of an approaching ship spreading among them.

Horne studied the horizon again, now feeling a breeze against his bare skin. But still he could not spot another ship. Below him, the crew was breaking into cheers as the sails began to flap, the limp moth-wings slowly coming to life. Babcock, Groot, Jingee and Kiro appeared at his side, as anxious about the approaching ship as they were excited by the rising breeze.

Horne's attention was caught by a distant serration. He passed the glass to Babcock. "What do you see?"

The four Marines took turns studying the horizon; Groot handed the glass to Jingee, saying to Horne, "*Schipper*, there is more than one sail."

"A bloody navy out there," growled Babcock, his eyes still swollen with sleep.

"Possibly a fishing fleet," answered Horne, but there was little conviction in his words.

Jingee passed the glass back to Horne. "The sails look slanted."

Cheng-So Gilbert had appeared on the quarter-deck behind the Marines. Horne handed him the glass, saying, "Give us your opinion, Mr. Gilbert."

The interpreter studied the approaching line of ships and said, "Praus."

"Praus?" repeated Babcock.

Cheng-So Gilbert kept the glass to his eye. "Narrow ships with reed sails. We spoke about them this afternoon."

"Sulu pirates," remembered Groot.

Cheng-So Gilbert surrendered the eyeglass to Horne. "There are many types of praus in these waters. The lateen sails of the Madrese. The square-sail outrigger from Borneo. The tilted double sails of the Sulu."

"Those are double," Kiro said, looking at the fleet drawing closer from the north-east, both extensions of its arms stretching back into the morning darkness.

"At an angle to the mast," added Groot.

Estimating that there must be more than fifty native craft in the approaching flotilla, Horne thought about running out the guns. The wind was rising too slowly to attempt an escape but the *Huma* could defend herself temporarily with cannon fire.

Sometimes, however, it was wiser not to aggravate an enemy. In rare instances it was ill-advised to put up a defence which stood no chance of success. How could they hope to win against such a horde?

"They must have been watching us all night," Jingee suggested.

"Waiting for a wind," said Babcock, now totally awake.

"Or for daylight to attack," added Kiro.

Babcock looked at Cheng-So Gilbert. "Are you certain they're Sulu?"

"There's not enough light to see the decorations which the Sulus paint on their boats."

"Look." Jingee pointed at the small navy.

Three boats were emerging from the line, the middle vessel no longer than a canoe, the two escorts topped with a pair of rectangular sails rigged at a forty-five-degree slant.

Studying the trio through the glass, Cheng-So Gilbert said, "They want to parley."

Horne ordered Jingee, "Get me my speaking trumpet."

The Tamil reappeared on the quarter-deck in only a few minutes, handing the trumpet to Horne as a man rose in the canoe across the water and called in a clear, resonant voice.

Cheng-So Gilbert listened and turned to Horne. "He wants to talk to the *nakhoda*, the captain of the ship. He speaks the Bugis tongue of the Sulu."

"Ask them to identify themselves," said Horne. "Where they come from. What they want from us."

Cheng-So Gilbert took the speaking trumpet and, holding the small ivory circle to his cherubic lips, called across the waves in a voice which sounded shrill in comparison with the deep tone of the Sulu spokesman.

Listening to the reply, Cheng-So Gilbert turned back to Horne. "They are from the Sulu islands of Lanani. They are looking for a ship which attacked a village on one of their islands. They say the ship belongs to the East India Company. Its leader is English."

"Tell them we are also looking for an East India Company ship. Tell them that the ship we are looking for is called the *China Flyer* but its 'leader' could easily have painted out the name."

As Horne listened to another exchange of words, he saw by the increasing light of day that each prau had cannon mounted on deck and directed on the *Huma*. Thank the Lord he had not attempted an escape. The

Huma would have been blasted to splinters and he and his men become food for the sharks.

"They say we must go with them and speak to their chieftain," Cheng-So Gilbert reported.

"Does he say where?" Horne asked. "Ask him. Try to buy time with more questions."

At that moment, praus were moving out from the end of the phalanx, surrounding the *Huma* in a breeze which had taken four days to appear. The Sulus had finished talking.

"What have you got us into now, wilful woman?" Jud complained to his wife. "I asked you for a breeze and you bring us pirates!"

Black legs wrapped around the topgallant yard, Jud clung to the rigging as the prau fleet sailed in close escort around the *Huma*. The crew had followed Horne's orders to weigh anchor and catch the rising breeze, but their excitement had abruptly given way to trepidation in face of the gathering Sulu fleet.

Jud's wife Maringa had been a household slave in Sheik All Hadd's Castle of the Golden Sand in Oman. Since she had died giving birth to their son, Jud had formed a habit of talking both to her and to the dead boy, in moments of joy as well as in fits of desperation.

Maringa gave Jud consolation. She assisted him. Her spirit and that of their son were with him night and day. They watched over him.

In the days immediately following their deaths, Jud had become a thief, looting and stealing, leading a shameful life, until the authorities apprehended him and gaoled him in Bombay Castle. Later, he attributed his arrest to Maringa's protective eye; it had been her way of taking care of him, of putting him back on the straight and narrow path.

Maringa's spirit had also led Adam Horne to Jud's cell, helped to free him from prison and make him a Bombay Marine. Maringa made life as happy for Jud as it could be without her and their son.

But what did Maringa have in mind now? Why could she not just blow him a little bit of wind from Heaven and be done with it?

"Perverse woman," he scolded at the sky. "Can't you once give me what I ask for? Do I always have to suffer for it?"

14

A Sulu Escort

The wind became so forceful throughout the morning that Horne ordered the sails to be trimmed to avoid overtaking the praus leading the Sulu escort. The native craft were swift but their mat sails made them less agile in a strong sea breeze than they were when it blew off the land. Careering across the silver-capped waves, they looked like fluttering brown sparrows escorting a mighty but graceful seabird.

The idea of breaking free from the pirate fleet tempted Horne but, mindful that the lead phalanx was a double-strong wall of Sulu praus, he suspected that the same notion had also occurred to them. To the north, south, and west, the single-file sentries kept their cannon trained on the frigate.

Yet he continued to toy with the idea . . .

Towards midday he noticed that six of the small tilt-sailed ships had fallen away from the rear escort. Where had they gone? Home to nearby islands? Would other praus be taking their place? Or perhaps more drop away?

He also noticed a headland rising in the south.

Chart in hand, he asked Cheng-So Gilbert if the island was Borneo.

Cheng-So Gilbert confirmed that it was. "That distant line on the horizon seems so dark because Borneo's coastline is dense with forest. They have few settlements there. I've heard the island referred to as 'the land beneath the wind.' That's because it lies below the path of the typhoon which blows from Japan."

"How populated are other parts of the island?" Horne asked.

"Borneo has no more than ten thousand people. They cluster mostly around the island's north-eastern points. Traders and fishermen. In settlements called Saba and Tungo and Bandar."

"The Sulu Sea lies to the east?"

"You are correct, Captain Horne. The Sulu Islands span the southern boundary of the Sulu Sea, like stepping-stones to the Philippine Islands."

The forenoon watch finished, Babcock, Kiro and Jud joined Horne and Cheng-So Gilbert on the quarter-deck; the three Marines listened as the Chinese interpreter described the local islands and talked about the diversity of their crops, ranging from tea to opium poppies. They were most concerned, however, about where they might be heading.

Jingee gazed northwards. "That's the South China Sea."

"Canton lies up there."

Jud pointed off the larboard bow. "So we should be heading *that* way instead of—" He pointed east. "—*that*."

Cheng-So Gilbert nodded. "If we had kept to our original plan, indeed, mister, we should be."

"But now we're sailing between Malaya and Borneo?" Kiro asked.

"Closer to Borneo, mister."

"That's Borneo you see to the south," added Horne.

"But if they're escorting us to the Sulus, we must go far beyond it."

The Marines' questions continued.

As he listened, it occurred to Horne that in any other circumstances this would be an ideal day: a few puffs of clouds dotting the blue sky; flying fish cutting across the bows of the ships; the wind capping the sea with silver foam.

"The Sulus are a short people," Cheng-So Gilbert continued. "They have the flat faces of the Bugis. Although small they are very ferocious."

"With the reputation of being pirates," Jingee contributed.

"Pirates and slave traders."

The announcement woke Jud from his reverie. "Slave traders?"

Cheng-So Gilbert waved at the escorting praus. "The Sulus control the largest trade in the Orient."

The Marines exchanged glances.

Gilbert continued, "Slavery was first introduced to these islands by the Arabs five hundred years ago. They came not only to capture the islanders but to sell slaves they brought from India and Africa."

Seeing the Bombay Marines shift nervously, Cheng-So Gilbert urged, "Do not fear. It is very rare for Sulus to sell *orang putih*—a white man."

"White man?" Jud beat his mahogany breast. "I worry about them selling a . . . *black* man!"

Cheng-So Gilbert hastened to reassure him. "No, no, no. Do not fear, mister. Do not worry. The Sulu Raja welcomes European ships. Nobody has anything to fear. The Raja will not take men off the ship of the great and powerful Honourable East India Company. Oh, no, no, no, indeed!"

Groot was not convinced. "What about the *China*

Flyer? Didn't that Sulu you talked to tell you that the
China Flyer destroyed one of their villages?"

"Yes . . ." Cheng-So's eyes were sharp and alert.

Gesturing to the forty-strong escort, Groot argued, "If
this fleet went looking for the *China Flyer* and comes
back home with us in tow, how hospitable is their Raja
going to feel to the East India Company then?"

Horne interrupted. "Do not speculate. Do not jump to
conclusions. Concentrate on what we know."

To stop the men worrying about slavery, he asked
Cheng-So what he knew about other islands, about the
Philippines, Molucca, the Dutch settlement on Java. The
Chinese translator gladly complied, squirming on his red
cushion at having upset the five men.

Towards the end of the afternoon watch, the wind still
held. Horne noticed that six more praus had dropped
from the rearguard. Their disappearance convinced him
that the time had come to voice his idea.

Sending Cheng-So Gilbert from the quarter-deck, he
stood with his back to the main deck and asked, "Men,
what do you think about making a break for it?"

Babcock thought he had misheard. "Try to cut loose
from these bastards, you mean?"

"It's highly risky, I know," admitted Horne, "and
could cost us our lives. But I think we can do it. How
do you feel about it?"

"I'm for anything," roared Babcock.

"Shhh. Keep your voice down. Behave as naturally as
you can. We must not arouse suspicions by talking here.
I'm certain we're under constant surveillance."

Babcock glanced cautiously around him. "Who from?
Where?"

"Perhaps every prau."

"Do you think so?" Babcock was wide-eyed.

"Absolutely," Horne insisted. "We must not appear to be making any plans, or doing anything out of the ordinary."

"What about the Chinaman?" asked Kiro. "Can we trust him?"

"It is my first instinct not to involve him in any plan. He might possibly warn or signal to the Sulus in some way."

"Why would he do that?" asked Babcock.

Kiro answered, "To save his own skin."

Babcock suggested, "Why not lock him in the hold?"

"My thought, too," confessed Horne. "But I decided against it. We shall need him later in China. We must not alienate him and lose any help he could give us."

He studied the three faces in front of him. "Before I begin telling you what I'm thinking, I want to remind you: the Sulus greatly outnumber us."

Babcock whispered, "But have you seen how many cannon each boat has? One!"

"My men can blow them to bits," Kiro said excitedly.

"More important, what about your men, Jud? Can they work quickly?"

"The men recruited in Madras are now as good as any crew from Bombay," Jud assured him.

"The men will do anything to get out of this fix," Babcock put in encouragingly. "They're all grumbling and scared about what's going to happen to them."

"Before we start anything," Horne stipulated, "I'll also have to talk to Groot and Jingee—if we are going to do anything. But it must be soon. When daylight begins to go, it goes quickly."

Reminding the men that they were undoubtedly being closely observed, he began describing how a trapped seabird could escape from a multitude of attendant sparrows.

●　　　●　　　●

Horne moved from his conclave on the quarter-deck to speak to Groot at the helm. Explaining how Babcock, Jud and Kiro concurred with his proposal to break away from the Sulu escort, he said, "The move will be dangerous and I won't proceed without total agreement amongst you men."

Groot's hands steadied the wheel. "I'd rather take a chance, *schipper*, than end up a slave."

"Slavery's not something you yourself are likely to have to worry about with the Sulus," Horne objected.

"I don't want slavery for anyone, *schipper*—me or a man with black skin like Jud."

"Then you agree to chance a break?"

"Aye, aye, *schipper*."

Horne explained the plan to him and then moved on to Jingee in the forecastle.

Jingee listened eagerly and was full of praise. "Captain sahib, you are indeed brilliant," he exclaimed. "We would all be stupid not to try such a plan."

"I won't act without every man's agreement, Jingee."

Jingee glanced guardedly at the crew. "These men, Captain sahib, will do anything to escape this—" He frowned toward the praus in the side escort. "—this trap."

"Babcock and Jud assure me of the same thing."

"I can go now, Captain sahib, and prepare them for the move and they'll do it. Believe me, I know, Captain sahib. I have heard them all worrying about what will happen to them."

"Do stress to them, Jingee, that the Sulus are most likely observing our every move."

"Count on their best co-operation, Captain sahib." Jingee promised. "They know the Sulus buy and sell men like animals."

He hesitated. "Captain sahib, may I ask you your opinion on one matter that's troubling me?"

"Of course, Jingee." Horne hoped the question wouldn't take long.

"It's about the Sulus. They claimed that the English ship fired on one of their villages. Do you think such a thing is true or do you think it's merely their reason for seizing us?"

Jingee's curiosity pleased Horne. He had been pondering the same question himself.

"It is my opinion, Jingee, that such an armada would not need an excuse to seize one solitary ship. Especially since they found us becalmed, virtually helpless.

"Secondly, we know little about the character of the man, Fanshaw, except that he's certainly one to take chances and is most likely avaricious; probably not someone who shrinks from violent measures. Such a person could have done such a thing."

"Why would he have fired on the village, Captain sahib?"

"My answer can only be guesswork. Plunder. Pillage. Fear of pursuit."

"So you think, Captain sahib, we are being made to pay for Fanshaw's crime?"

"Remember, we do not know if the man who supposedly gunned their settlement was indeed Fanshaw. But whoever it was, or why they did it, the Sulus want to punish some English ship for the act. I must confess, too, that I think they have good cause. But we have our own cause, Jingee," Horne reminded him. Patting his shoulder, he urged, "Let's work well—and quickly—to make the most of our plan."

The word continued to pass round.

15

Breakaway

The brilliance of the blood-red sunset pleased Horne as much as the fresh wind. Perhaps the early evening's beauty—coupled with the *Huma*'s submissive behaviour throughout the past twelve hours—had lulled the Sulus into a false sense of security. He hoped so.

The praus in both side escorts were close enough for Horne to hear laughter drifting across the water, and to smell the pungent aroma of smouldering charcoal. Were the crews preparing an early evening meal? Did that mean they were not planning to put into port soon, but would press on until they reached whatever Sulu island was home to them?

Aboard the *Huma*, Horne saw his men idling near their stations, waiting for his command. Kiro's gunners lounged in small groups on deck, their eyes glancing nervously back to Horne for the signal to run out the guns.

Horne maintained his calm pose. Preparations had gone on so unobtrusively that he was certain even Cheng-So Gilbert had no suspicions of an imminent escape attempt. At the moment, he was below in his cabin, presumably recording the Sulu captivity in his journal.

Lingering by the rail, Horne smiled as he noticed that two more praus had fallen away from the rear escort. The *Huma* obviously enjoyed their captors' complete and utter trust.

Cautioning himself not to become over-confident, he nevertheless felt more light-hearted than he had since leaving Fort St. George. More pleasing than having decided on the escape was the fact that his Marines, and all hands aboard ship, had unanimously agreed with the plan. Every last man was willing to take a desperate step to avoid the threat of being enslaved. Besides, what was the point of living if one never took chances?

Babcock climbed the ladder. "All's ready," he reported, voice low, eyes anxious.

Horne, clasping his hands behind his back, maintained his casual bearing as he made a last-minute appraisal.

The hands aloft were waiting. The gun crews looked from Horne to Kiro and back to Horne. Jingee's white turban bobbed near the forecastle.

Resting his weight on one leg, Horne looked over his shoulder for one last check on the escort.

Six praus lagged in the wake; the side guards were less than a half-cable away, north and south.

Horne looked fore. The lead phalanx had relaxed in formation, the first line lagging into the second.

Satisfied, he tilted his head back, filled his lungs with fresh air and said, "Babcock, this is it."

Babcock chuckled. "See you on the other side, Horne."

Horne faced the main deck, glanced momentarily to the left escort, and bellowed, *"Wear ship!"*

The men leaped into action. Hands raced for the braces. Yards swung in the wind; blocks screamed, and the deck reared from the fury. The helm went over with a lurch, leaving the wind rushing at the stern.

"Man the lee braces," called Horne over the scream of rigging, eyes darting back to the jib boom swinging in the sudden arc.

"Prepare to fire—" he cautioned. *"—at will!"*

Kiro shouted the crews to their guns as Jingee dashed along the gun decks, fire buckets in both hands, followed by his barefoot brigade bearing water and sand.

"Don't go for a broadside," insisted Horne. "Fire at will. *Fire* at will. FIRE AT WILL!"

In the ship's abrupt change of tack to the north, the larboard guns blasted at the enemy's rear escorts; Kiro concentrated the starboard guns on the leading praus, four cannon alternating fire as the crew sponged and reloaded ball on top of round shot.

To the east, the praus struggled to follow the change of tack, but the Marines' cannon fire, and the native vessels' inability to meet the wind, spread the Sulus into instant disarray.

Through clouds of smoke, Horne caught sight of a figure staggering from the companionway. Cheng-So Gilbert. The interpreter stared in horror at the smoke and confusion around him. Groping to steady himself, he tried to attain his balance but the cannon sent forth another volley and he went sliding across the deck.

Horne's attention was diverted to an explosion across the water. A few seconds later the deck shook beneath his feet.

The Sulus had scored their first strike. But there was no time to worry about damage. He looked fore as the prow speared its way through the enemy line, Sulu cries drowning the smashing of wood, the ripping of the praus' palm-mat sails.

Kiro's guns recoiled a third time. Worried about the enemy's response, Horne raised the spyglass and saw

through the smoke that the lead praus were still struggling to make their stays.

Another impact shook the deck.

The strike had hit the larboard—from the praus which
had been lingering to the rear.

Looking astern, Horne saw the side escort's shot
splashing in the sea, unable to make its mark.

The wind strong at her stern, the *Huma* sped onwards
through the wreckage of the northern escorts, through
men clinging to boards and bits of mat sail.

It had worked! The flock of brown sparrows was left
behind in disarray as the big seabird swept away from
their circle.

Relieved and triumphant, the crew broke into abandoned shouts and cries, hugging one another, waving
bandanas, ripping off the *dhotis* from their loins to fly
them high in the rigging, wildly slashing the cotton strips
back and forth as they danced on deck.

Horne's face creased into a smile as he witnessed the
hands' jubilation. Raising the spyglass to his eye, he was
gratified to see the Sulu praus floundering in disarray to
the south.

Babcock slapped his back. "You crafty old fox, Horne.
You did it."

Jingee was still anxious. "Will they catch us, Captain
sahib?"

"They're too tangled," answered Horne, studying the
distant confusion through his spyglass. "The praus changing course are careering into one another."

Babcock filled his lungs with fresh air, booming, "This
wind at our arse will soon put the miles 'tween us, too."

Horne was indeed grateful for the fresh wind that blew
them northwards. Wondering what lay ahead, he swept
the horizon for any sign of sail. They now had to concentrate on the purpose of the mission—overtaking the
China Flyer.

16

Macao—The *China Flyer*

The **China Flyer** approached Macao through a channel less than a mile wide, guarded each side by a squat fort. The roadstead beyond was crowded with boxy fishing junks, European merchantmen tilting at anchor, sampans with central awnings. There were canoes and rafts among the sampans, paddled by men, women and children noisily hawking fruit, vegetables or poultry, shrilling their availability to do laundry, sew clothing or provide love.

Lothar Schiller stood on board the *China Flyer*, sipping a cup of bitter tea in the dank morning as he appraised the ramshackle wooden houses and rickety bamboo moorings dotting the swamps. The gilded crosses crowning the distant Catholic missions did nothing to alter his impression of Macao as one of the ugliest, most uninviting settlements he had ever seen.

A tapping against the deck attracted his attention. He turned but did not immediately recognise the man approaching him.

Attired in a raspberry-silk frock-coat and powdered wig, George Fanshaw wobbled towards Schiller in high-heeled court shoes, tapping an imperious ivory staff against the deck as he walked.

Mein Gott! Does this fool think he looks like a gentleman? Schiller fought to suppress a howl of laughter as Fanshaw advanced towards him in the foppish outfit.

Flicking a lace handkerchief, Fanshaw ordered, "Neither you, Mr. Schiller, nor the crew shall go ashore in Macao."

"How long do we stay here?" asked Schiller, and forced himself to add, "—Herr Fanshaw?" He must try to remain respectful until Fanshaw had paid him his money.

"I go now to seek the Hoppo's permission to proceed up the Pearl River." Raising his hand, the wrist heavy with ruffled lace, Fanshaw pointed to a copper-roofed building across the harbour. "I'll need a boat to row me to their offices, Mr. Schiller."

Schiller nodded, muttering, "Aye, sir," and turned to execute the order. He had little reason or desire to linger in conversation with Fanshaw.

"Do not allow anybody aboard ship in my absence," Fanshaw called after him.

Schiller paused. "Not even Manchu officials?"

Fanshaw patted a large pocket on his frock-coat. "I am going to take care of the officials now."

Schiller understood. "I hope you save something for me."

"You'll get your share when we reach Whampoa, Mr. Schiller."

More loudly, he called, "Make certain no enemies come aboard ship, do you hear? You're to consider everybody an enemy, understand?"

Schiller's tea had turned cold by the time he returned to his position. Emptying the cup over the side, he saw the oarsmen bending their backs in unison as they rowed Fanshaw through the harbour congestion.

Watching the wherry move through the sampans, rafts

and canoes, he wondered: Did Fanshaw have reason to worry about enemies attacking him? His biggest fear was still that the East India Company would send the Bombay Marine after him.

Schiller faced the grim truth of his situation: whether he liked Fanshaw or not, he would have to protect him against any and all rivals if he was ever going to get paid.

At the age of ten, Lothar Schiller had been hired out by his father as a cabin boy to the Prussian merchant ship, the *Melanchthon*. After sailing back and forth from the North Sea to the Baltic, he learned on his return to Hamburg that his father had died in his long absence, and that his mother had married a Hanoverian apothecary, leaving no word of where her son could find them.

Lothar Schiller had grown up under many flags. Hanoverian. Austrian. Prussian. He had lived, too, in many towns. Bremen. Cassel. Hamburg. Consequently, at the age of thirteen he felt no loyalty to any king or country, only a kinship to the race whose language he spoke—German.

Finding himself homeless, Schiller had lied about his age in order to fight as a mercenary foot soldier with the French Army commander, Maurice de Saxe, against the Duke of Cumberland's Allied Army in Flanders. Knowing little about the War of the Austrian Succession, and not caring to know, he only worried about the money pouch he would receive as his soldier's pay.

Attached to the Irish Brigade under de Saxe, Schiller met British soldiers of fortune who taught him his first words of English. He learned, too, that careers could be made in Europe's professional armies.

Fired by the hope of joining such a force, he travelled

to England, but there was no market for his services at that time. Instead, he signed on with a succession of merchant ships plying between England, Scotland, and Denmark. As much at home on the sea as he had been on land, he quickly graduated from deck hand to helmsman's mate, making friends with men below decks as well as with young officers.

Then came a chance to sail to Madras aboard the HEIC Indiaman, *Castle Bukeley*; Schiller seized it, secretly hoping to find work in India as a mercenary soldier in the struggle between the French and the English. He disliked the orderliness of Company merchantmen and longed for the rough-and-tumble life of soldiers for hire.

Although the Seven Years War had not officially ended in Europe, fighting had ceased in India by the time Schiller arrived at Fort St. George. Rather than return to England on the Indiaman's home voyage, he signed on with Company ships trading between the East Indian islands.

Work proved to be scarce, an increasing number of Lascar sailors taking jobs usually reserved for European seamen. Schiller spent months unemployed, scouting for work in Madras's Black Town.

In February of this year, he had heard a rumour of employment being offered by an Englishman organising a private venture to China. He had several meetings with Fanshaw, convincing him of his ability both to command a ship and to keep silent about the voyage. The promise of gold influenced his decision to work for the unlikeable man.

The harbour noises of Macao brought Schiller's attention back to the present. Looking in the direction where Fanshaw's boat had disappeared through the crowded sampans, he regretted having taken this job on the *China*

Flyer. The advantage of being a mercenary soldier was that a man seldom met his employer; it was easy to fight for a king you neither loved nor hated. But Schiller knew that he had actually come to detest George Fanshaw.

17

Macao—The *Huma*

Six days north of Borneo, Jud sighted a mountain peak breaking through the low-hanging morning clouds.

As the *Huma* skimmed across the westerly edge of the South China Sea on the briskly holding winds, a rocky coastline became visible off the larboard beam. Excitement about a landfall brought men running to the side and, as they watched, twin mountain peaks appeared on the north-west horizon.

On the quarter-deck, Cheng-So Gilbert told Horne, "The Chinese call those two mountains—" He held a stubby finger to either side of his round head. "—asses' ears."

Jingee spotted boats clustered against the shoreline.

The Sulu pirates still fresh in Babcock's mind, he asked, "Damn! Do we have to run out the guns?"

Studying the vessels through his spyglass, Horne saw that the centre of each long, low boat was spanned by a low cabin.

"Sampans." He passed the spyglass to Groot. "Totally undisturbed by our presence."

Cheng-So Gilbert agreed. "The Chinese have little curiosity about foreigners. They're probably fishermen out for the day's early catch."

Small islands, clusters of grey rock stubbled with pale green moss, dotted the coastline as the wind carried the frigate on its north-eastern course towards the Pearl River estuary. As the sun rose higher in the east, Horne estimated that they would soon be approaching the river mouth and decided that it was time to change his clothes. Governor Pigot had strongly impressed upon him the importance of turning out properly attired on this mission. He must look like a true officer of the Honourable East India Company when he presented himself to the Hoppo in Macao.

Fresh linen, brightly polished boots, immaculate breeches and frock-coat awaited Horne in his cabin. A basin of hot water stood ready and, tying back his hair, he began to shave, inwardly dreading the loss of the freedom he had enjoyed in the past weeks. Bare-footed, his shirt open to the waist, he had basked in the day-to-day comfort of being a Bombay "Buccaneer" rather than a stuffy, overdressed "Marine."

The days when they had been becalmed, even the brief but threatening captivity by the Sulu islanders, in retrospect seemed preferable to dressing in his uniform and confronting the Imperial representatives of the Manchu court. But, then, had not the happiest periods of his life always been the journeys between two ports? Seldom the departure, certainly not the arrival.

Planning how best to present himself to the Hoppo, Horne decided to take only Cheng-So Gilbert ashore with him. A personal escort of Marines would be impressive, certainly, but only if they were smartly dressed in uniforms decorated with gold braid and high-standing collars. Horne's five prized men would impress the Chinese as being nothing more than a pack of tatterdemalions in their bare feet and *dungri* trousers. The Lord only knew what the arrogant Portuguese would make of the motley Marine unit arriving in Macao. Horne hoped to avoid all contact with them.

There were practical reasons for not taking the five Marines ashore. This was not the end of the mission and, needing a crew for the return voyage to India, Horne wanted every Marine and seasoned hand to guard the recently recruited men from abandoning ship. The chances of supplementing his crew in China were negligible.

A knock on the door disturbed Horne's meandering thoughts. Turning from the small looking-glass where he had been studying the results of his razor, he opened the door and was surprised to see Jingee standing outside.

The morning meal had been served. There had been ample hot water for shaving. And Horne was certainly not like the officers of His Majesty's Royal Navy, who required a man to help them dress.

Bowing, the diminutive Tamil asked, "Is everything to your satisfaction, Captain sahib?"

"Perfectly, Jingee." *What the devil . . . ?*

Jingee's small black eyes darted past Horne into the cabin. "Shall I give your coat one last brushing, Captain sahib?"

"No, Jingee. It's quite satisfactory." *What does he want?*

Dropping his eyes to his bare feet, Jingee hesitated. "Captain sahib . . . Will you be wishing *me* to go ashore with you in Macao?"

"No. I'll take Mr. Gilbert."

"Oh . . ." Jingee's eyes remained on the cabin floor.

He was jealous. Of course, that was it. How stupid not to have noticed the signs before now. Jingee prided himself on being secretary, personal servant, *dubash* to

Horne. But since leaving Madras it had been Cheng-So Gilbert who had spent long hours with Horne on the quarter-deck and at dinner, explaining Chinese customs, commenting on the charts, describing ancient ways and traditions.

Determined to dispel all this foolishness, Horne ordered firmly, "You shall stay aboard ship, Jingee, while we secure a pilot to take us up river."

"Yes, Captain sahib."

Horne explained considerately, "I want you to see that no man goes ashore, Jingee. We cannot completely trust our new recruits from Fort St. George."

"You're always most cautious, Captain sahib."

"You can also add to our stores, Jingee, if you see anything that might make the crew's table more enjoyable. They deserve a treat."

"I have money, Captain sahib, from what you gave me in Madras."

"If there's any left from that, you might see if you can get some wine for my table."

Disheartened, Jingee turned and went up the companionway.

The rowing-boat inched through the press of harbour craft, Cheng-So Gilbert crouching behind Horne, pointing to the tiered roofs of the Portuguese Governor's Palace, the ancient Monkey Shrine surrounded by a tangled swamp, the golden crosses of the Jesuit mission gleaming high above the fetid harbour.

The Portuguese had established themselves in Macao two hundred years earlier, explained Cheng-So Gilbert, interrupting his historical monologue to shriek at the vendors paddling alongside Horne's boat. They carried bamboo crates of live chickens, earthenware casks of rice beer, multi-shaped baskets of white gourds, bean cakes, pastries, long, strange-looking cabbages.

More sampans crowded the distant docks; the din of squealing pigs, barking dogs and chattering voices floated across the grey-black water. Beyond the boats, lines of rickety hovels faced the harbour, a few of the buildings fronted with English signs, among them, "The British Inn."

Macao was crowded and dirty and insalubrious. Horne wondered how much of this congestion and filth was intrinsically Chinese, how much the influence of Portuguese settlers.

The oarsmen had propelled them across the narrow-mouthed harbour and were approaching a squat building roofed with copper. Cheng-So Gilbert tapped Horne's shoulder, drawing his attention to a column of soldiers marching along a wide pier; the end was dominated by six green bronze cannon facing the inlet's mouth.

"The Office of the Imperial Hoppo," explained Gilbert and ordered the oarsmen to make for the brass-inlaid steps extending from the pier down into the murky water. The column of marching soldiers had halted and at the top of the steps stood an official, tawny face impassive beneath a small cap fastened under his chin by a black silk cord.

After an exchange with the officer, Gilbert motioned Horne to precede him up the steps.

Horne grabbed the hand rail and stepped out of the boat, surprised that the officer did not offer a greeting, not a flicker of salutation. Was this a hint of the reception awaiting him in the office beyond?

Taking a deep breath, he looked towards the end of the pier and saw a pier of tall black lacquered doors, flanked by guards in long black cloaks, their hands rest-

ing on the hilts of gently curved swords. Behind him, the
other guards fell into position.

Horne walked authoritatively towards the doors, the
leather heels of his boots echoing on the wooden pier,
while Cheng-So Gilbert's black satin slippers softly pad-
pad-padded at a respectful distance behind him.

The lacquered doors opened as Horne approached.
Passing into an entrance hall, he was pleased when Gilbert came up beside him and called to two men simply
garbed in plain robes, approaching from the opposite direction.

Horne produced his documents from the pocket of his
frock-coat. Cheng-So Gilbert took them and, bowing,
passed them to the robed men.

"Captain Horne, you may wait here." He pointed to a
sliding rice-paper door.

The chamber beyond had no furniture. The lighting
came from a window high on a white wall. The only
decoration was a Manchu dragon painted on gold silk.

Alone in this spartan room, Horne paced the wooden
floor as he considered for the first time the possibility of
the Hoppo refusing the *Huma* permission to proceed up
river to Whampoa. How should he plead his case? Could
he turn to the Portuguese for support? Had other East
India Company ships arrived from England before the
monsoon? Would they be in Whampoa?

Horne disliked the total impotence that travellers suffered in strange lands. Even after being based in India
for eight years, he frequently felt isolated there by the
barriers of language and custom.

Compared with China, however, India seemed bright,
colourful and welcoming. China reminded him of the few
Chinese water-colour paintings he had seen—pale, man-
nered, intrinsically cold.

Another difference was the people. Indians were by

nature an out-going lot, anxious to meet foreigners, quick to exchange stories and customs, and to laugh. But the Chinese appeared to have none of that Asian curiosity. Did they truly consider Europeans to be barbarians? If so, had it always been this way, or only since the recent overthrow of the Ming Dynasty by the northern Manchu? Were there benefits from such aloofness?

Did the Chinese insulation protect them from foreign domination? India was eager to sample new and different ways; but perhaps that was why foreigners like the East India Company could make headway into the country's very government. Was India vulnerable because of her people's genuine friendliness?

Horne wondered if he would have to return here to-morrow . . . and the next day . . . and the next. Would he be kept waiting to see some oriental martinet who would scrutinise him and ask him to repeat answers to irrelevant questions?

The clank of metal sounded in the distance.

The rice-paper door glided smoothly to one side and Cheng-So Gilbert entered the room, both hands tucked into the wide sleeves of his jacket, round face beaming.

"Will he see me now?" Horne disliked the anxious sound in his voice.

Gilbert bowed respectfully. "Your business is settled, Captain Horne."

"Settled?"

"I have learnt the answer to your question."

"The *China Flyer*'s arrived?"

"Eleven days ago. The Hoppo gave the chop to an Englishman named George Fanshaw to progress up river to Whampoa."

So he was on the right trail. But what about the date? Fanshaw had reportedly left Madras in March. What had happened in the intervening months? Why had the *China*

Flyer arrived in Macao only eleven days ago?

Stepping aside, Cheng-So Gilbert bowed to Horne, motioning him out of the room.

As Horne emerged into the outer hall, he saw no armed escorts waiting for him, no emissaries to lead him to an inner office.

He looked back at Gilbert. "When does the Hoppo interview me?"

Reaching into one sleeve, Gilbert produced Horne's documents, along with an unfamiliar scroll, saying, "The Hoppo's satisfied by what he read. You have received Imperial permission to proceed up the Pearl River."

"What about the *cumshaw*? The gift?"

Cheng-So Gilbert pointed through the open doors. "The Hoppo's guard have already begun attending to that matter."

Outside, Horne saw three war junks surrounding the *Huma* across the harbour. Was that why they had kept him waiting so long, to unload their gift?

"What's happening?" he demanded.

"The Hoppo's sent his ships to collect the *cumshaw*, Captain Horne."

"But I gave no permission for anyone to board my ship."

"Captain Horne, the Hoppo takes no more than his share."

"Mr. Gilbert, did you give the Hoppo's men permission to go aboard the *Huma*?"

"Captain Horne, this is China. Nobody has to give the Imperial Hoppo permission."

Horne roared, "How in bloody hell do they know what I want to give them?"

Cheng-So Gilbert explained patiently. "You seek permission to proceed to Whampoa. The Hoppo granted you his chop. For that privilege he takes a *cumshaw* which is tallied by the percentage of the ship's cargo and the extent to which he wants the *Huma* searched. The guards assured me they would not be aboard long." He smiled. "That is the Manchu way, Captain Horne."

Horne could not hide his anger, but he saw the irony in the situation. He had dreaded today's interview with the Imperial officers and now, when he learned that he did not have to meet anyone, he was losing his temper. But he felt he was in the right. He had heard endless stories about Manchu etiquette, Manchu protocol, Manchu formality; but they had stuck him in a waiting-room while they sacked his ship!

"Excuse me, Mr. Gilbert," he said, "but in my opinion, the Sulu pirates were more civil towards us than the . . . Manchu!"

18

The Pearl River

While Jingee laid out supper on the desk, Horne reread Governor Pigot's orders. The trip north from Macao had begun at midday, a slow trek up the winding Pearl River with no breeze to fill the sails, so that they were dependent on the tow-lines of the oared escort boats.

Earlier, in Macao, Jingee had purchased chickens and vegetables from the sampan vendors. He had stewed Horne's supper over a galley fire and now, as he served the tasty meal, he chattered about the morning's events.

"When the Chinese came aboard ship, Captain sahib, I thought our men were going to dive into the water. They were so frightened, Captain sahib. Everyone thought the Chinamen had come to rob and kill us or take us away at sword-point."

"Ummm," responded Horne noncommittally, spooning up the chicken stew, his attention focused on the instructions which Governor Pigot had given him concerning the respect to be paid to Chinese officials—how to *kowtow*, how to fall on your hands and knees on the floor and tap your head in front of the honoured person's slippers.

Jingee filled Horne's glass with the rice wine he had purchased in Macao, continuing, "I didn't know what to do when I saw the Chinese rowing towards the *Huma* in their junks, Captain *sahib*."

"Ummm," repeated Horne, folding Pigot's letter and setting it aside on the desk. He could not imagine the porcine governor ever falling to his hands and knees in front of any official, Chinese or otherwise. He appreciated that respect must be shown to foreign officials but did not believe that he could ever prostrate himself before any autocrat.

"Who was there to understand the language they were shouting at us?" Jingee went on. "Remember, Captain sahib, that the interpreter had gone ashore with you."

"Of course."

Allowing Jingee to chatter on, Horne reached for the ledger of cargo records he had left open beside his supper tray. He should be excited by the Hoppo's report that George Fanshaw and the *China Flyer* had arrived at Macao and preceded the *Huma* up river; a confrontation might take place very soon. But for the moment he was concentrating on trying to understand the Chinese procedure of etiquette and gift-giving. Tomorrow the Co-Hung in Whampoa would also expect a *cumshaw*, and Horne intended to be prepared for them. He did not want to depend totally on the recommendations of Cheng-So Gilbert.

From the desk, Jingee turned to tidying Horne's cabin. "One Chinaman counted everything on beads, Captain sahib—ping, ping, ping. He snapped little green jade beads on a silk thread, counting the chests they carried from the hold."

The Hoppo's men had taken eleven chests of opium from the *Huma*, leaving a balance of seventeen. But as yet Horne had no figures from Babcock to indicate how many bolts of Madras cotton the harbour officials had taken as part of their *cumshaw*.

On the other side of the cabin, Jingee was gathering up laundry, complaining, "What right have they to come and take what they want when they can't even explain why they're doing it?"

Horne reminded Jingee as he copied figures from the ledger, "Mr. Gilbert says it's the Manchu way."

"Mr. Gilbert." Jingee sniffed disapprovingly. "I would like to know how much of a percentage Mr. Gilbert receives from the Hoppo."

Horne's pen hesitated on the paper. He had not considered that aspect. Did Cheng-So Gilbert receive a percentage of a *cumshaw*? Hmmm. He must ask.

A round moon hung low in the sky, illuminating the towlines strung between the *Huma* and the rowing-boats, and making their hemp cables look like the silvery strands of a spider's web. The night's stillness was broken by the steady splash of the oars in the eddying waters, and the rhythmical chirrup of cicadas in the tall grass bordering the Pearl River.

Jingee knelt in the ship's heads, scrubbing Horne's laundry as the frigate inched up the river. Thankful that he was not on tonight's late dog watch, he was using the time to finish the work he had been prevented from doing earlier today in Macao, when the Chinese had boarded the *Huma*.

Still angry about the intrusion, he was fretting, too, about Cheng-So Gilbert. The Chinese could not be trusted, he decided. The Chinese were shifty, he told himself. Cunning. They smiled while they plotted intrigues against you.

Jingee's cousins in Riau conducted a pepper trade between India and China. They had told him about the disingenuous Chinese, and how the merchants of Canton cheated, lied and stole in their bargaining with them.

Jingee rinsed soap ash from the clothes with fresh drinking water as he considered the growing importance of understanding foreign customs. More and more ships were sailing to distant lands nowadays, and travellers must be prepared to learn the codes of conduct they found there—whether or not they approved of them.

Jingee had always been curious about other people's ways. His interest had led him to learn languages, and his ability to speak a diversity of tongues and dialects had enabled him to find work as a *dubash*—a secretary and translator. Before becoming a Bombay Marine, he had been employed by an English factor in Hyderabad, a man with no respect for local mores, who one day had yoked a man of the *Brahmin* caste to a lowly *Panchama* and set them to work ploughing his garden. Jingee had pleaded with the Englishman not to defile the high caste man by attaching him to an untouchable, but the foreigner had scoffed at Hindu law and ignored the appeal. Jingee had had no choice but to slit the Englishman's throat.

Memories of the murder reminded him of the knife he had used earlier tonight to prepare Horne's supper.

As he wrung out the clean clothes in the moonlight, Jingee pictured the scarlet necklace he would draw around the neck of Cheng-So Gilbert if the pudgy Chinaman betrayed Captain Horne sahib. He would slit his throat as easily as he had butchered the plump chicken.

Jingee knew, too, that, deep within him, his distrust for Cheng-So Gilbert stemmed from a jealousy that the Chinaman spoke so many more languages then he did himself.

•   •   •

While Jingee laboured under the moonlight, in his cabin
below Horne was pushing a glass of rice wine across his
desk to Cheng-So Gilbert as he asked, "Do you receive
a share of the *cumshaw* I gave to the Hoppo in Macao,
Mr. Gilbert?"

Cheng-So Gilbert replied without hesitation, "I receive
a share from the mandarins in Whampoa."

Horne raised his wine-glass and both men sipped the
golden-yellow wine, Horne aware that Gilbert had not
answered the question.

"Excuse my dullness, Mr. Gilbert, but I still do not
understand the procedure. Did the Hoppo in Macao also
give you a share of my *cumshaw*?"

"The Hoppo is an Imperial office, Captain Horne," Gilbert explained patiently, dabbing the corners of his cupid
lips. "It is beneath the Imperial officers to give gifts to a
common linguist such as myself. I receive a percentage
from the Co-Hung merely because they are mandarins—
men involved in trade."

"So to all intents and purposes you receive a percentage because it is similar to a commercial transaction."

"In China, Captain Horne, *cumshaws* do not fall into
the category of percentages, taxes or gratuities. They are
tokens of respect."

"But tied to the value of a ship's cargo or its inspec-
tion?"

"That is frequently the case, yes, Captain Horne."

Pleased that Gilbert was answering the questions so
readily, Horne continued, "Will the mandarins in Whampoa give you part of the cotton and opium they receive
from me?"

"Such an arrangement, Captain Horne, would not be
unusual."

"Can you specify to them what commodity you would
prefer? Cotton or opium?"

"I would prefer opium, of course. There is always a ready market for poppy tar in China. But the mandarins will make the decision."

Horne recrossed his booted feet beneath the desk. "Tell me about the mandarins, Mr. Gilbert."

"Mandarins are the leading merchants in China, Captain Horne. The Emperor formed them into the Co-Hung. They are beneath the Hoppo in rank, but many men are now whispering that they are gaining too much power. Some predict that they will soon control the Imperial throne."

He added, "Already the mandarins have allowed the opium trade to grow to an extent which the Emperor greatly disapproves."

"Opium is not indigenous to China, is it, Mr. Gilbert?" Horne said. "What is its history here? How did it become such a key import?"

"Many years before your disciple Christ was born, Captain Horne, opium was brought to China by holy men from India. They travelled the country, impressing people with the endurance of their meditation and abilities to pray for long periods of time. They cured sicknesses with mysterious powers unknown to the Chinese. When the local priests learned that the foreign holy men's strength came from opium, they, too, began exploring the magic of the poppy tar."

"So religion introduced opium to China."

"To the Buddhist and Taoist priests, yes, Captain Horne. From them, members of the Ming Court discovered that opium vapours held in the lungs could induce luscious dreams. Through the courtiers, the practice filtered down to the populace."

"By this time were the Chinese trying to grow their own poppies?"

"The Chinese indeed tried cultivating poppies, Captain

Horne. So, indeed, did a few islands where the practice
had also spread—the Philippines and Sulus. But the bulk
of it still comes from the clement districts of India. To
this day, opium is one crop which the mandarins do not
pay for in porcelain or silk. Opium has come to be valued
so highly by the Chinese people, that the foreigners know
they can demand payment in silver. There are even special warehouses for storing opium chests arriving from
abroad."

"These warehouses are in Canton?"

"Some. But the main opium depot is called Kam-Sing-
Moon. It is an island beyond the mouth of the Pearl
River."

"Is the entire opium trade controlled by the government?" Horne sipped at the wine.

"That is the Manchu wish, Captain Horne. But the
mandarins have been greatly troubled lately by illegal
trade conducted by small merchants along China's southern coastline. The territory is too vast for total control
and the Manchu fear that foreigners will go to those small
traders. The monopoly would be in great jeopardy. The
Manchu jealously protected their monopoly and condemn
all illegal traders to the Dragon Prison in Canton."

The conversation ended on a sombre note, with Cheng-
So Gilbert explaining how opium had eventually become
the ruination of the Ming Dynasty. Horne thanked him
for the evening's enjoyable companionship and, after bid-
ding him good night, decided to take a breath of fresh
air before ending his day.

On the quarter-deck, he found Groot and Babcock on
the last dog watch. Babcock was grumbling about the
slow progress up river, Groot jabbering nervously about
the possibility of the Chinese ambushing them in this
defenceless position. "I feel like a tied pig, *schipper*," he
complained.

Horne had weighed the likelihood of being entrapped by the Chinese as they were towing them up the winding Pearl River. The snail's pace would leave little or no way of escape; the guns would be useless against clamouring assassins. But what alternatives did he have? To keep the crew armed and alert would definitely offend the Chinese. To have waited at the river mouth for the *China Flyer* to return down river from Whampoa would have been another possibility, but how long would the wait have been? Fanshaw might have heard of their presence and escaped overland. A third alternative would have been to leave the *Huma* in Macao and travel up river in a native vessel. But Horne saw such action as little better than abandoning ship to the enemy at sea.

Saying goodnight to Babcock and Groot, he descended the companionway and made the round of hands playing dice in small groups around the deck. They thanked him for the rice beer he had paid for in Macao and talked about China, the visit from the Hoppo's guard, the night's journey up river.

"Captain, sir, this beer must be the best thing in China," said a sharp-faced Javanese. "May the gods all smile down on you for your kind generosity."

"I've been to China as a boy, Captain," bragged a short man from the Philippines. "Most of the people there are as poor as a wharf rat. But the rich ones, sir, they have money to loan God."

"Excuse my humble opinion, Captain, sir, but have you thought of letting us man the rowing-boats up river?" asked a muscular young Mauritian.

Horne listened to each man, then, telling them to finish their dice games before the next watch, he bade them goodnight and returned to his cabin.

The moonlight was streaming through the stern windows. Horne lay on his bunk and listened to the cicadas'

serrated chorus. His conversation with Cheng-So Gilbert
had reminded him of how, years ago, Elihu Cornhill had
discussed the use of poppy tar in warfare: opium, he had
said, could be as effective as physical torture in obtaining
vital information from captives. Men often mumbled secrets they would never divulge in a normal state of mind.
Some men, too, feared the hypnotic sleep that opium in-
duced and readily answered a captor's questions rather
than be made to suffer the drug's effect, a form of torture
in itself.

His eyes heavy with fatigue, Horne felt himself slipping into unconsciousness, his mind becoming hazy, his
thoughts disappearing like clouds. At the back of his
mind he wondered if the feeling was similar to opium's
initial effects.

Suddenly, he heard noises above him.

Sitting upright, he grabbed for his sword, looking for
his breeches as there came sounds of running on deck.

At the same moment, the door crashed open and the
cabin filled with men in black hoods. In the bright moonlight Horne saw that they carried the same curved blades
as the Hoppo's guard in Macao.

19

Co-Hung

In the panelled chamber of Whampoa's Hall of the Moon Wind, a slender man with a flat Manchu face, seated in a rosewood armchair, was talking to the Englishman George Fanshaw. Abutai, the Co-Hung's chief mandarin, wore a long string of amber beads over his pale green robe and spoke in slowly enunciated Chinese.

"The Co-Hung wishes to continue trading with the Honourable East India Company after we welcome the new ships you promise to send us from England, Mr. Fanshaw. Therefore," he stressed, "we do not wish to inflict harm on any person affiliated with the East India Company, not even those men called the Bombay Marines whom the Maritime Guards captured last night on the Pearl River."

Abutai had informed Fanshaw at the start of this morning's meeting that an Englishman and his crew had been seized last night and were being held prisoner at an undisclosed spot here in Whampoa.

Fanshaw remembered to follow Chinese etiquette as he replied: "Excuse me for speaking in your illustrious presence, noble Abutai, but the Bombay Marines do not

belong to the East India Company. Not in the same way
as do officers aboard Company Indiamen. Marines are
mere brigands and cut-throats. They are recruited from
prisons. They are retained as a man keeps a dog to guard
his house from strangers."

Abutai kept both hands tucked into his embroidered
sleeves. "An officer's uniform was found in the captain's
quarters. There were also instructions from Governor Pigot of Madras to the captain—Adam Horne."

Chinese protocol frequently bordered on the ridiculous,
as Fanshaw had learnt during his many visits to China,
but he easily and quickly adapted to an obsequious role.
His difficulty now was finding out whether the Company
had sent the Bombay Marine in pursuit of him. How
could he discover what crafty Abutai had learnt from
reading Horne's orders?

"Despite my unworthiness to be in your esteemed presence, great Abutai," he began, "I can only suggest that I
offer my services to read the written orders and tell you
if they are authentic or false. I do not know this man,
Adam Horne, whom your Guard arrested last night. But
I suspect his mission is not what it seems. Could it be,
Your Excellency, that he has come to China to make
contacts for the East India Company with the independent merchants trading illegally along your southern
coastline?"

The chief mandarin's angular face remained stony.
"You presume to know a great deal about China, Mr.
Fanshaw, by speaking about illegal trade on our southern
frontier."

"Abutai so eminent, if an ignorant man such as myself
knows about those cursed merchants plying an illegal
opium trade against the noble wishes of the Imperial Co-
Hung, how many other foreigners must know the same
fact? Including Governor Pigot. I can only hint to you,

learned great one, at the way the East India Company could profit from not one but *two* trading sources with China. Not only with the Co-Hung but with the lowly coastal merchants. It would not be the first time that England has dealt with contraband."

The mandarin considered Fanshaw's syrupy words. "There was also an interpreter travelling aboard the Marine ship, Mr. Fanshaw. He upholds the captain's story about being in search of your ship, the *China Flyer*."

Damn it! So his worst fears had come true. The Bombay Marine were here in pursuit of him. And the Chinese knew.

Fanshaw also cursed his oversight in not realising that Pigot would send someone to translate for the Marines and the Manchu officials.

Boldly, he replied, "As always, you are gracious as well as erudite, great Abutai. I am forever indebted to be reminded that the East India Company will try to frustrate my every move. Humble as I am, every word I say to you poses a great threat to their monopoly of the rich China trade."

Then, more hesitantly, he said, "If the eminent Abutai wishes, my humble service could be of even greater use to his far-reaching power. I could interview this interpreter travelling with the Bombay Marines . . ."

Unmoved by the proposal, Abutai answered, "Before such a thing can happen, Mr. Fanshaw, the Co-Hung wishes you to appear once more before them."

Bowing deeply to the mandarin, Fanshaw just restrained himself from dropping to a complete *kowtow*. "I am honoured to appear again before the august body of the Co-Hung. I consider it my duty to disclose all I know about the cur-like soldiers, the Bombay Marines."

"The Co-Hung will want to hear about other matters as well. Particularly about the new company of English merchants you are proposing to introduce to China."

"O eminent Abutai, I shall tell the Court of the Co-Hung the same facts that I am and have been honoured to tell you—that the new board I represent from London is sounder than the East India Company. Its chairman, Sir Jeremy Riggs, until recently represented the Company's pepper trade. He has told me that he has grown tired of the Company's duplicity. The presence of the Bombay Marines here in Whampoa attests to the Company's treachery. Next they will be sending in troops to attack the Chinese. You have no reason to fear military action from the gracious gentlemen whom I am representing to you."

"Further debate is needed, Mr. Fanshaw," Abutai insisted, "before the new English trading company is put on the Co-Hung's privileged list."

"Excuse such presumption, Your Grace, at raising such a question in your presence. But earlier in this audience which you are charitable enough to grant me, your lofty Eminence said that the Maritime Guard seized the Bombay Marines last night on the Pearl River. I was too stupid to understand whether the Marine's ship had appeared on the Hoppo's privileged list or had stolen unawares up the Pearl River."

"Captain Horne requested permission from the Hoppo in Macao to proceed up the Pearl River. He presented the Hoppo with opium. Suspecting that the Marine might be here for ulterior reasons, the Hoppo accepted the *cumshaw* and allowed him to proceed."

Fanshaw was wondering why Abutai was divulging such facts to him when, unexpectedly, the chief mandarin added, "Do you think the time will come, Mr. Fanshaw, when there are as many spies in trade as there are in warfare?"

What did the mandarin mean? Was it a veiled Chinese

warning? Fanshaw had no time to ponder it. There were too many other questions in his mind.

He tried again. "The military protection of your water-ways greatly impresses me, illustrious Abutai. Is it difficult to take custody of a European ship here in Whampoa, while the captain remains in command?"

"The Marines' ship will not be kept in Whampoa."

"Ah, there is more opium aboard!" It was a gamble but Fanshaw wanted to know. "The Marine's ship will be taken down river to Kam-Sing-Moon and unloaded at the depot. Of course."

The flicker of annoyance in Abutai's dark eyes told Fanshaw that his observations were going beyond the permitted limits.

"That is no concern of the Marine commander, Adam Horne," said the mandarin. "Captain Horne need only contemplate a future in the Dragon Prison of Canton."

The Bombay Marine captain gaoled! The idea thrilled Fanshaw.

"Your cleverness should not surprise me, Your Eminence," he exclaimed, "but I constantly marvel at the shrewdness of your mind. Yes, by imprisoning the leader of the Bombay Marine in the Dragon Prison, you will show the East India Company that they must not take lightly the Imperial Co-Hung. The great Manchu powers act on their own volition. They are not a court to be intimidated by the East India Company."

Fanshaw's mind worked quickly as he savoured the idea of Horne being imprisoned. The East India Company would never jeopardise their position with the Chinese to rescue a lowly Bombay Marine. They would probably not even risk insulting the Chinese by negotiating for Horne's release. The Company was anything but loyal to its men. There was also the time factor. Fanshaw's new trading company would soon be incorporated and in operation.

But the alternative would also benefit Fanshaw. If the Company did try to save Horne and were stupid enough to rescue him, the action would corroborate everything Fanshaw had said, that they had no respect for China or the Chinese.

Fanshaw resumed his obsequious style. "High Abutai, if I cannot be of use to you by interviewing the Marine's interpreter, perhaps I can offer my humble talents to speak to the Bombay Marine Captain, Adam Horne."

The chief mandarin surprised Fanshaw by promptly agreeing. "A meeting might be arranged in the next few days. But it must be soon because Captain Horne will appear next week in front of the Co-Hung."

"On trial?" blurted out Fanshaw, forgetting all about etiquette.

The doors opened at the far end of the hall. Abutai rose from his armchair and Fanshaw knew that he had gone too far in his questions.

Hoping to redeem himself by the ultimate form of respect, he fell to the floor in front of the chief mandarin, hands out in front of him, haunches in the air, and knocked his forehead one, two, three, four, five times on the thin silk carpet spread before the dais.

Above him, Abutai proclaimed, "You shall receive word as to when and where you can interview Captain Horne, Mr. Fanshaw. Be waiting at your rooms tomorrow for the Co-Hung's instructions."

When Fanshaw raised himself with the help of his ivory staff, he saw only the back of the chief mandarin's robes floating behind him as he departed from the panelled room.

•   •   •

Fool of a barbarian Englishman. Abutai moved swiftly down the corridor from the Hall of the Moon Winds, thinking how like rodents Englishmen were, running this way and that when they saw their ambitions becoming endangered. Fanshaw's offer to visit Adam Horne in his prison provided Abutai with a convenient excuse to detain the former agent in Whampoa.

The Co-Hung had yet to decide about putting Fanshaw's new British trading company on the Privileged Merchants List. Abutai slowed his step, wondering how the council would react to the news that Fanshaw possessed knowledge of local merchants trading opium illegally along the country's southern coastline. Only a stupid barbarian would divulge that he possessed such valuable information, especially someone proposing to send trading ships to China.

Approaching the copper doors of the Co-Hung's Jade Chamber, Abutai decided that, most certainly, fate had delivered the Bombay Marine captain to him to use in dealing with George Fanshaw. Yes, he would allow Fanshaw to visit Adam Horne in his prison tomorrow.

20

The East Seas Trading Company

The London spring had yet to appear that year. In a cold drizzle falling for the seventeenth consecutive day in May, Sir Jeremy Riggs stepped out of the Honourable East India Company offices in Leadenhall Street, and looked up and down the row of narrow houses in search of his carriage. Seeing no sign of it, he raised his eyes to the clock on Plunkett's Buttery opposite the East India Company. He had only ten minutes before he was due in Whitechapel; he would have to walk the twelve streets to his destination. His cloak would be soaked, his boots mired when he got there, but he could not be late for the meeting.

Hearing the thunder of horses' hooves to his right, he turned and saw a carriage rushing towards him from Aldgate. He stepped back to avoid being splattered.

In front of the East India office, the driver reined in the frothing beasts. A red face with shaggy grey eyebrows appeared like an apparition at the carriage window, ordering, "Get in, Riggs."

Benjamin Cowcross was the last person Sir Jeremy Riggs wanted to see, particularly here, in front of Company headquarters.

"Get in out of the rain," repeated Cowcross, throwing open the carriage door. "Ride with me to Whitechapel."

Without even leaving word for his coachman that he had gone on, Sir Jeremy climbed into the carriage and slammed the door, urging, "Tell your driver to move on, Cowcross! Move on! We must not be seen together. Not here. Not yet."

Cowcross laughed at the baronet's concern, his ale-foul breath filling the carriage as he scoffed, "You're too cautious, Riggs. Too damned cautious. Everybody in the City will know soon enough you're doing business with me. And that you're a richer man for it. Our new company is going to take the cake out of the mouths of your fancy cronies at the East India Company. Mark my words. We're on to a pot of gold, Riggs."

Sir Jeremy sank into the opposite corner of the rumbling carriage. Public knowledge of the fact that he was in partnership with Ben Cowcross, the manufacturer of iron manacles and collars for the slave trade with the American colonies, was precisely what he did not want. He was associating with Cowcross only because he was too poor to partake in commercial ventures sponsored by the East India Company.

Less than an hour after Sir Jeremy had left Leadenhall Street, he was sitting in cramped offices in Whitechapel with the five men who formed the board of the new East Sea Trading Company. The smell of rancid suet drifted in from an adjoining pie shop, and a serving girl scuffed around the low-ceilinged room, handing out pewter tankards from a tray as she eyed each man.

At the head of the table presided Josiah Creddige, the portly heir of a Liverpool merchant whose fortune was based on hand-painted chintzes imported from India.

Creddige the younger hoped to double his inherited fortune by bringing silks from China.

To Creddige's right sat David Potter, a hatchet-faced broker of coffee. Potter was anxious to capitalise on England's growing taste for China tea and was already negotiating for larger premises in St. James's.

Nicholas Kidley, a short man with a face covered in warts, was sitting on the opposite side of the table. His successful apothecary business depended on oriental spices and herbs; an increased supply of camphor, cloves and opium—all the oriental ingredients that composed his nostrums and potions—would enable him to expand his activities.

Next to Kidley sat swarthy David Thistle who owned the shipyards in Deptford renowned for building swift frigates sold to privateers. Thistle had ambitions to expand into the lucrative business of merchant shipping. He was offering his yards—as well as financing—to build the first merchantman for the East Sea Trading Company.

Beside Thistle sat Sir Jeremy Riggs, his worried face and refined tailoring making him appear out of place among this group of ruthless businessmen. Sir Jeremy had inherited his baronetcy and a manor house, but little money to support the style of living that went with them. Through social connections, he had won a sub-licence from the East India Company to import pepper from Bantam; but on going out to the Indies to oversee the venture, he had quickly found he hated the life there and had returned to England ill and on the verge of bankruptcy. In London, he had thrown himself on the mercy of Ben Cowcross, who had willingly loaned Sir Jeremy money on his manor house to finance the Bantam adventure. But after investigating the baronet's financial situation, Cowcross had discovered that his most valuable possession was not the house but the licence to import pepper to

England. With characteristic cunning, Cowcross had devised an intricate scheme by which Sir Jeremy could retain his family seat and make a fortune for himself. All he had to do was take five partners into a complicated, and not wholly legal, trading adventure.

Seated at the opposite end of the table from Josiah Creddige, Cowcross asked the first question of the day's meeting. "Riggs, have you spoken recently to your friend the Duke of Turley?"

"Of course." Sir Jeremy disliked the way Cowcross ignored his title. "He's waiting to hear if the Chinese Co-Hung will grant us permission to trade in China before he presents our case to the Crown."

"And when we stuff money into his purse," said Cowcross.

"That, too," answered Sir Jeremy.

The only salve for Sir Jeremy Riggs in this uncomfortable situation was that men like the Duke of Turley also needed money and were prepared to do business with such rogues. The Duke had lost his own fortune on an East India Company convoy which the Company had failed to insure properly. Turley still carried a grudge against the Company's Board of Directors and, for revenge as well as profit, was willing to help secure a Royal Charter from his hunting partner, King George, for a rival trading company to import goods from the Orient. But the Duke would only act when the new company had proof that they could trade with the Imperial Co-Hung of China.

"Any news of the *China Flyer*?" asked Creddige from the other end of the table.

"It will be at least another three months before George Fanshaw returns to England," answered Sir Jeremy.

As the meeting had been called for the purpose of obtaining a progress report from each member, Sir Jeremy himself now asked a question. "What's the progress on the *Charity Bourne*, Mr. Thistle?"

The shipbuilder answered with confidence. "We're keeping to the estimate of twenty pounds per ton on the *Charity*, Sir Jeremy. Two pounds cheaper than the Thames Company builds for the East India Company."

He turned to Cowcross. "Have you sold all your shares?"

Like the East India Company, the East Sea Company divided shares in a voyage into thirty-two lots. All shares in the new company's first voyage had been purchased by the five businessmen at the table, who in turn, had sold them at profit to family and close friends. Sir Jeremy was promised fifteen per cent of the profit for his part in the venture.

"What word do we have on insurance?" asked Potter the coffee merchant.

Cowcross snorted. "The blackguards at Lloyd's Coffee House are as jittery as titmice about going against anything or anyone challenging the East India Company!"

Horrified, Sir Jeremy sat forward in his chair. "You've not told anyone yet about our new company, Cowcross?"

"Nay. I know how to keep my hat on my head, Riggs. I'm no fool. But I sounded out them Lloyd's coffee guzzlers enough to know they'll remain loyal to the old company. But don't you worry about insurance. I lied about dumping fifty niggers overboard on an Atlantic Crossing two years ago, so City Assurance owes me a pretty favour. The *Charity Bourne* won't sail without proper insurance."

Kidley the apothecary said, "But Sir Jeremy is right. If the East India Company catches a whiff of what we're doing, Cowcross, they'll slap us all in irons as traitors for plotting against the Company's Crown Charter."

He turned to Sir Jeremy. "Have you got your Company licence renewed?"

The baronet nodded. "Renewal was granted to me this very day, I'm pleased to say."

"Did the Company ask any questions?" inquired Thistle.

"No," answered Sir Jeremy. The licence to trade in Bantam was a cover for the building and fitting of the merchantman. "So far nobody has shown any interest in my plans."

"Any questions about how you raised the money to renew your licence?" Cowcross's eyes danced beneath his thick brows, enjoying the execution of the plot he had laid.

"I mentioned to the Court of Directors that I'm contemplating taking on partners."

"Did they ask who those gentlemen might be?"

"The licence allows me partners, and I assure you, Mr. Cowcross," Sir Jeremy added quickly, "there will be no problem on my part. Especially when the Duke of Turley intervenes on our behalf with the Crown."

"Yes, back to Turley," said Thistle. "When do we meet him?"

"As I said, sir, the Duke of Turley is waiting to hear whether we obtain China's permission to trade."

"And he gets his money," repeated Cowcross.

The apothecary, Kidley, interrupted. "It's all very fine to be concerned about Crown approval. But the important side of this venture still remains the Orient. Let us fret not so much about the Duke of Turley as about George Fanshaw in China. Did he make his escape from Madras? Is the Company pursuing him? What are his chances with the Chinese?"

A momentary silence fell over the table.

Cowcross belched. "George Fanshaw. Damn right.

He's the key to this puzzle. But I said it before and I will say it again—I don't like the man. I know, I know. I introduced him into our group. But he's a rat. No better than a rat that crept out of the mire."

There was a general murmur of agreement round the table. George Fanshaw was not a likeable creature. The only dissenter was Sir Jeremy Riggs, and he kept his peace, musing on how ironic it was that these five should pass judgement on a man little different from themselves—uncouth, uneducated, rough upstarts in the world. But, then, were the shareholders and board members of the Honourable East India Company any better? No. The difference lay in the fact that the directors of the East India Company—and their families—had been involved longer in the lucrative oriental trade. They had had time to marry into the aristocracy, buy titles from the Crown, cultivate the patina of the gentry. Some day Thistle, Creddige, Potter, Kidley—even coarse Ben Cowcross—would take their own places within England's titled society.

The meeting continued.

PART THREE
The Clash

21

A House Guest

"Have you received word, dear, from that nice Captain Horne?"

The question jolted Commodore Watson from the cat-nap he was enjoying on the verandah of Rose Cottage. Sunday afternoons in Bombay were sedentary. Following morning service at St. Andrew's, there was little to do but pay calls on other English families or sit at home behind one's own white walls, hoping that no callers would pull the bell at the front gate and demand to be entertained.

Two months had passed since Adam Horne had left Bombay. In that time Commodore Watson had received word from Governor Pigot in Madras—via Governor Spencer in Bombay—that Horne had arrived at Fort St. George and left again in pursuit of the *China Flyer*.

In the past weeks, Watson had recovered from his at-tack of *coup de soleil*. His health had begun to mend just in time for the arrival from London of his wife's niece, Emily Harkness, for a year's stay at Rose Cottage.

Having received no reply to her question, Mrs. Watson repeated, "Have you heard, dear, from that nice young

Captain Horne? I'm planning a party for Emily and would like to begin compiling the guest list." She raised her head from her embroidery.

"Horne? What about Horne?" Watson stretched in his deep cushioned chair. Since his indisposition he had been sleeping far too much. Quiet Sundays at home did little to help the lingering lethargy he suffered as an after effect of his illness, but it was too hot to take a walk out-of-doors to keep alert, and pacing through the cramped cottage made him feel like a caged animal.

"I want to invite Captain Horne to a party," Mrs Watson went on in a louder voice. She had noticed that something seemed to have gone out of her husband since his illness; nowadays he seldom paid attention to what she said and even the testy bark had all but disappeared from his voice. Had he not yet fully recovered? Or was this new apathy merely a sign that old age was taking its toll? The only consolation was that he had not returned to his gin-drinking.

Mrs. Watson turned to her niece. "Captain Horne's a very agreeable young man. A good family, too, I understand."

Trying to involve her husband in the conversation, she called across the tiled verandah, "Merchant bankers, aren't they, dear?"

Watson squinted at the book he had taken from the table in an attempt to stay awake. "What's that?" he asked.

"Captain Horne's father," repeated his wife. "Isn't the father in banking?"

"Horne walked away from the bank. Turned his back on a fortune."

"I'm asking because I want to reassure Emily that all young men who come out to India are not rogues and cutthroats."

Watson glanced at the girl arranging a sheaf of drawings on the table in front of her. "Looking for an eligible match?" he teased.

Twenty-year-old Emily Harkness was slim, with blonde hair softly curling around her oval face. In the past three weeks her complexion had become a soft brown, despite the protection of a parasol; she was proving to possess a surprising—almost masculine—ability to withstand the Indian heat.

Studying the pen-and-ink drawings spread out in front of her on the wicker table, Emily answered, "I have no immediate plans, sir, for marriage. Nor for any other contract restricting my freedom."

"Hmmmph. That does not surprise me," replied Watson, reflecting that the girl would be a real tomboy if she weren't so damned pretty, and as content pottering around the house as she was when she was out exploring the city.

Emily Harkness was both a blessing and a worry to her aunt and uncle. She went sight-seeing with groups of other young ladies, but she was equally happy poking through marketplaces and bazaars with her sketch pad, as interested in local faces and costumes as she was in seeing Bombay's ancient shrines.

"Don't plan any gatherings for me," she insisted as she lifted a drawing of Elephant Rock from the collection. "You know how I hate society."

"Don't say you *hate* society, dear," scolded her aunt, troubled by the girl's modern use of strong words.

"Let us say, Aunt, that I don't feel the need to meet people every hour of the day. I'm quite content with my own company."

"But, dearest," protested Mrs. Watson, "you have travelled a great distance to broaden your outlook. Certainly that includes making new friends."

"I am making many new friends. The Truscotts. Hannah Starett. The Catchpole sisters."

"All young ladies," observed the diminutive Mrs. Watson.

"I dare say, Aunt. Most of the men I have met here seem to be interested in one thing and one thing only—marriage."

Watson peered over the top of the leather-bound volume, more interested in the women's conversation than he was in the subject of his book—the social consequences of billeting Caesar's troops during the Gallic campaigns.

"Adam Horne is certainly not interested in marriage," he contributed.

Emily Harkness crumpled her drawing of Elephant Rock and stuffed it into the pocket of her smock. "Then, perhaps, sir, I should meet this mysterious Captain Horne. Men with marriage in mind never say what they mean—until after the wedding."

The Watsons exchanged glances.

Miss Harkness continued, "Yes, I do believe I should enjoy making the acquaintance of a man who might say what he means without fearing that he will frighten off a potential helpmate."

The girl had a mind of her own; that was as certain as her exceedingly pleasing appearance. Emily Harkness definitely enlivened a dull Sunday afternoon at Rose Cottage. But as for the advisability of introducing her to Adam Horne . . . Would these two headstrong people prove incompatible? Commodore Watson wondered. Or worse perhaps: would two social misfits like these merely reinforce the independent spirit in one another? Such a thing would be catastrophic for both man and woman.

22

The Imperial War Junks

Eighteen yellow oars rose and fell in silent precision, propelling a long, slim rowing-boat away from the wharf in front of Whampoa's Inn of a Thousand Pearls, and moving through the floating vendors towards the *China Flyer* heeling at anchor in the afternoon wind. George Fanshaw sat rigidly in the stern, looking from the frigate lying directly in front of him to three Imperial war junks silhouetted against the far shore. He was paying two calls today: the first on his captain, Lothar Schiller; the second on the war junks which served the Imperial government as temporary prisons.

Twenty-four hours had passed since Fanshaw had spoken with Abutai, the Hoppo's chief mandarin. In that time he had considered various courses of action and had decided on what he considered to be the safest, most foolproof way to secure the establishment of his new trading company in China—and ensure his own personal safety.

A hail rose aboard the *China Flyer* as Fanshaw's narrow rowing-boat approached through the floating vendors. Lothar Schiller appeared at the side, shouting for his men to hurry and lower the ladder for their visitor.

"I did not expect you until tomorrow, Mr. Fanshaw," he greeted his employer at the port entry.

Fanshaw passed in front of Schiller impatiently fanning himself with his blue silk tricorn hat, as he ordered, "Let us speak alone."

Schiller followed him to the foot of the quarter-deck ladder. "Bad news, Mr. Fanshaw?"

Fanshaw spun round indignantly, spitting, "Did I not say the Bombay Marines were on our trail, Schiller?"

"The East India Company?"

Fanshaw's eyes moved to the three Imperial war junks across the harbour, but he held his tongue. Why tell Schiller more than he need know about the Bombay Marines and their whereabouts?

Guardedly he replied, "The Hoppo's patrol captured the Bombay Marine two nights ago on the Pearl River. I learned it yesterday from the chief mandarin, Abutai."

"Does this change your plans, Mr. Fanshaw?" asked Schiller.

Fanshaw replied icily, "To the extent that I want you and the *China Flyer* out of Whampoa by nightfall. I can escape overland if events suddenly turn against me. But I want the *China Flyer* free to sail for England when I give the order."

Plans had indeed gone wrong for Fanshaw; Schiller could see it in his face as well as understand it from his words. Common sense told him, however, that close-lipped Fanshaw was not the man to confide many facts to him.

"Shall I have trouble leaving here?" he asked, looking around the harbour for patrol boats that might detain him. The only suspicious vessels were the three junks which had arrived yesterday and remained isolated offshore from the stilted pier houses.

Fanshaw stepped closer to Schiller. "Our cargo will provide you safe passage. The Hoppo accepted the *cumshaw*. Abutai agrees that you should deliver it in its entirety to the depot."

"The opium?" asked Schiller, increasingly intrigued by Fanshaw's air of mystery.

Fanshaw nodded, glancing at the idling crew, fearful of spies and eavesdroppers. "I've arranged for you to deliver the chests to Kam-Sing-Moon beyond the mouth of the Pearl River."

"I can sail back down to Macao?"

Producing a document from inside his frock-coat, Fanshaw explained, "Here's your permission to sail. Take your time unloading the cargo. Wait for me off the island. I'll be there one way or another by tomorrow night."

"Sir, there is one important matter we must first settle."

Fanshaw pulled back indignantly. "What do you mean?"

"The matter of pay."

"Pay?"

"You said, sir, you would pay me in Whampoa."

Fanshaw exploded. "Good God, Schiller, this is hardly the time or place to start badgering me about money. Haven't you been listening to a word I've been saying? There's a new change of plan, man!"

Schiller raised his voice in turn. "When *will* you pay me?"

Glancing back at the surrounding crew, Fanshaw lowered his voice. "Wait till I see you at Kam-Sing-Moon," he promised.

Schiller stubbornly crossed both arms across his chest. "You do not pay me now, Mr. Fanshaw, I do not sail from Whampoa."

Fanshaw mopped the perspiration from his brow. "I certainly do not have the money on me now. Be sensible.

Do you want to risk the Chinese seizing this ship, so that you will be stranded in China? Is that what you want?"

He was right. Schiller hated to admit it, but there was logic in Fanshaw's words.

Determined to get his money, however, he raised his fist, threatening, "You do not pay me at that opium island, Mr. Fanshaw, you will regret it. I promise you that. You will regret it very deeply."

Fanshaw went on his way to pay his second call. The rowing-boat sped towards the three reed-sailed vessels, skimming more quickly over the dark, filmy water once the oarsmen were free of the clamouring sampan vendors. The boat slowed as it reached the second junk, Fanshaw calling in Chinese that he carried the Co-Hung's permission to board the Imperial vessel.

Two sentinels in black cloaks emblazoned with a red dragon waited at the top of the rope ladder. Fanshaw produced a document and announced haughtily in fault-less Chinese that he had come to speak to their English prisoner.

One of the sentinels called to a guard seated in a group on the junk's high poop-deck. The man who came to-wards them wore a leather tunic and helmet and a large ring of keys dangling from a thick belt round his waist. He studied Fanshaw's document and, satisfied as to its authenticity, beckoned him to follow, making for the cabin on the junk's main deck.

The guard unlocked the low, iron-banded door and Fanshaw asked him to wait outside, since he wished to speak to the prisoner alone. Inside, he saw a lean man seated cross-legged in a pallet stretched beneath the low windows to one side of the door.

"Adam Horne?" he asked.

"Whom do I have the honour of addressing?" asked Horne, not rising from the pallet.

Fanshaw studied Horne. The Marine was confident and self-assured, handsome in a rugged, wind-burned, buccaneer manner. But his accent was educated, obviously the product of wealth and good breeding. Certainly no run-of-the-mill, rough-and-tumble Bombay Marine. Not the man Fanshaw had expected him to be.

"Why have you come to China, Mr. Horne?" he demanded.

"If you know my name, sir, you have apparently read my orders." Horne still wore the breeches and shirt he had grabbed when the hooded raiders had surprised him aboard the *Huma*.

"Documents are easily forged, Mr. Horne," Fanshaw reminded him, enjoying the power he held over a man born to the class to which he merely aspired.

Governor Pigot's description of George Fanshaw fitted this pinched-faced, self-important, over-dressed Englishman. Horne was certain he was Fanshaw. He decided that the man must enjoy the favours of the Chinese Hoppo if he was able to visit him aboard this floating prison.

He challenged him. "I sailed from Fort St. George on a mission for the East India Company and it is proceeding exactly as I expected."

"Indeed, Mr. Horne, do your orders include being arrested and imprisoned?"

"My orders, sir, are to find you."

"Me?"

"George Fanshaw. Servant of the Honourable East India Company."

Horne's certainty amused Fanshaw. "If I am the man you claim you are looking for, Mr. Horne, what do you propose to do now that you have found me?"

"You sail aboard the *China Flyer*, do you not, sir?"

Horne nodded towards the row of windows behind him, and the English frigate beyond.

"From?"

"Madras."

"Destination?"

"Whampoa."

"Reason?" Fanshaw appeared to be amused by this verbal fencing.

"You have come to China, Mr. Fanshaw, to secure a place on the Hoppo's Privileged Trading List for a rival trading company."

"Rival to whom, Mr. Horne?"

Horne was working on the theory he had developed since leaving Fort St. George. "Sir, the only Britons chartered to trade with China are the Honourable East India Company."

"If I were here for such a reason, Mr. Horne, why should I be sailing a Company ship?"

"That, sir, is precisely the reason I am taking you back to Madras."

Fanshaw laughed. "Ah, so you sail in convoy, Mr. Horne. That, or you expect reinforcement soon to help you take the *China Flyer*."

"As you know from reading my orders, sir, the *Huma* sails alone."

"If you intend to take the *China Flyer* unassisted, Mr. Horne, you are either a very able seaman or a fool."

"Perhaps I am both," said Horne, adding, "Like Lothar Schiller."

Fanshaw's eyes dulled with anger. "For a man who thinks he knows so much, Mr. Horne, you know very little. Perhaps I should tell you how little you know.

"First, let me inform you that your ship, your beloved *Huma*, has been taken down river to Kam-Sing-Moon. The Hoppo is unloading your cargo of opium at the storage depot there. But your *cumshaw* will buy you no privileges, Mr. Horne, as Governor Pigot obviously intended. The Hoppo has decided you are to be moved to an Imperial prison—after your trial."

He smiled triumphantly. "Perhaps it would be more fruitful to speculate about your own future, Mr. Horne. You can prepare the defence you will give to the Hoppo's council when you appear before them next week."

"Your scheme will never work, Fanshaw," Horne said unexpectedly from the pallet. "No matter how well you think you have laid your plans, you will never succeed."

Fanshaw turned away abruptly. He rapped on the iron-banded door, calling, "Guard! Open the door, guard. The interview is over."

Horne jumped to his feet, insisting, "The East India Company will never let you rest, Fanshaw. Don't be a fool. There'll be other men following me. You're a wanted man, Fanshaw."

The door opened; the two Chinese sentries in black capes entered the cabin, the gaoler standing by the door with his keys.

Horne moved towards the Company agent. "Where are my men, Fanshaw?" He pointed to a junk anchored between him and the shore. "Are they out here, too? Awaiting trial?"

From the doorway Fanshaw answered, "Mr. Horne, the only thing you should concern yourself with is the defence you must give to the Hoppo next week for presenting false documents in Whampoa."

"Where are my men?" Horne repeated, fists clenched at his side.

The guards stepped forward, pushing him back towards the pallet.

Half-in, half-out of the doorway, Fanshaw called over his shoulder, "Wherever your men are, Mr. Horne, let's

hope for their sake that they are being more sensible than
you."

The door slammed in Horne's face.

How much of what Fanshaw had said was true? Had the
Huma really been taken down river to the opium depot?
Was the Hoppo indeed planning to move him to a prison
on land? Would he have to defend himself against allegations of presenting false documents in Macao? Or was
it all a fabrication that Fanshaw wanted him to believe?
Horne paced the cabin after the agent's departure, his
thoughts in turmoil.

Fanshaw had divulged nothing about himself, he realised. But the mention of Lothar Schiller's name had an-
gered him. Why? Had there been a rift between the two
men?

Horne ran one hand through his tangled hair, his
thoughts jumping to his Marines.

He looked to left and right out of the cabin's double
line of narrow windows. Were the men imprisoned in one
or both of those other boats? Or had they been taken
down river aboard the *Huma* . . . if there was any truth in
that story.

Horne had last seen his men the night before last, when
the Chinese Black Hoods had dragged them and Cheng-
So Gilbert from the *Huma*, hurling them into one barge
while they threw Horne into another and then brought
him blind-folded up river. The crew had been left aboard
ship.

Horne sank onto the pallet. He knew that the sensible
thing to do was to prepare a defence for the Hoppo's
council . . . He tossed restlessly. Was that story, too, a red
herring? Did Fanshaw want him to concentrate on one
point so that he would ignore more important possibili-
ties? Was the man as clever as Horne assumed him to

be, or was he crediting him with too much guile and cunning?

One thing was certain: the scoundrel had courage. Fanshaw was challenging the largest, richest company in the history of the world. Whether for his own advantage or for the benefit of others, Fanshaw had singlehandedly tackled the might of the Honourable East India Company.

23
Prison

Aboard the largest and outermost of the three war junks, Groot peered through a crack in the planking of the hold. As the rich purples and reds of the setting sun streaked across the harbour, he strained his eyes to see the activity aboard the distant European frigate.

"She's weighing anchor," he reported to Babcock, Jingee and Jud, waiting anxiously behind him. "She's going back down river."

"Can you see the name on her prow," whispered Jud in the near-darkness.

"She's the *China Flyer*," answered Groot. "I'm certain of it."

"Any more sign of that fop Fanshaw?" asked Babcock.

The men had been taking turns watching the harbour activity since the rowing-boat had carried a white man in a frock-coat and tricorn hat out to the frigate. His second stop had been the junk anchored to the east of their own. Although they could not see Horne aboard the adjacent ship, they were certain he was imprisoned there. Last night and early this morning they had seen the yellow glow of a lantern inside the cabin on its main deck and a man pacing back and forth, someone who looked very like Horne. They were certain, too, that the white man in the frock-coat, who had visited the frigate and then the junk, had been George Fanshaw.

"Did Fanshaw's boat take him back ashore?" Jingee asked.

"I can't see any more," complained Groot. "The light's changing too quickly and too many sampans have come this way."

As the sun had started its descent towards the distant pine forests, sampans had begun venturing out across the oily black water towards the Imperial junks, selling fish, vegetables and arrack to the seamen for their evening meal. A few boats, more brightly painted than the others, carried women who the men had guessed were the courtesans called "flower women," coming to the war junks to entertain the Hoppo's guard.

Groot waved his hand, eye to the crack. "The *schipper*'s lit his lamp again."

Babcock reminded him, "We don't know if that's Horne over there."

"It's the Captain sahib," said Jingee. "Why else would Fanshaw have gone there?"

"To speak to the guards."

"No, it's the Captain sahib," insisted Jingee. "I can recognise him a hundred miles away. Nobody paces back and forth, back and forth like the Captain sahib."

Behind them, Kiro crept aft from the hatch, reporting excitedly, "The grille's not locked into the frame. The peg slides."

"What about guards?" Babcock asked.

"There's a clear view of them all seated on the poop deck. They're eating and drinking and getting very friendly with the women."

"If you can get a clear view of them, they sure in hell

can get a good look at the hatch," Babcock said.

"Perhaps, but—" Kiro shook his head. "They're too busy with their supper and the girls."

Babcock was still unconvinced about their plan to escape from the junk. "Fine," he conceded. "Suppose we manage to climb out of this stinking hold. What do we do then?"

"Swim ashore and get boats."

"Kiro's right," said Jingee. "Those sampans clustering around now makes a perfect cover for us."

Babcock pulled his big ear. "I don't know. It seems pretty daft. Escaping to shore then stealing boats to come right back out here again to get Horne."

He nodded at Cheng-So Gilbert sitting forlornly on a bolt of hempen rope. "And what about the Chinaman?"

"He goes with us," said Kiro.

"What if we gag and tie him and leave him behind," Jingee suggested. "That would keep him from making a noise and giving us away while we escape."

"Why would he do that?"

"He's Chinese," said Jingee disapprovingly.

"He's also in gaol with us," Kiro argued.

"He could be a spy."

"He could also divulge what he's heard if we leave him behind."

Jingee remained unconvinced. "I don't know. I don't trust him."

Babcock suggested, "Let's find out once and for all how much we can count on him."

He leaned forward, beckoning to Cheng-So Gilbert, and whispered, "You. Come over here."

Cheng-So Gilbert crawled reluctantly towards the small group crouched in a circle. His clothes were ripped and soiled from the journey up river in the prison barge.

"Can you swim?" whispered Babcock.

Quick, deep nods.

"You sure? From here to the shore?"

"I learned to swim with the Jesuit fathers," he whispered.

"Another reason not to trust him," whispered Jingee.

Cheng-So Gilbert took a deep breath and closed his eyes.

"Give him a chance," said Babcock, then continued his questions.

"Would you prefer to stay aboard here?"

Cheng-So Gilbert gasped. "While you go ashore?"

Babcock nodded, saying to the others, "That means he's heard us talking about our plans."

Groot intervened. "Perhaps he can help us. He knows this harbour. Maybe he can tell us where to get boats."

"It's never going to work," Cheng-So Gilbert warned them. "The surrounding wharves are dangerous, not only because of the Hoppo's guards and the soldiers but also because of the wharf people who will recognise you immediately as strangers."

He leaned further, whispering, "The wharf people will do anything for money. Rob, steal, slit your throats, betray you to the authorities. They are the lowest of human life. Thieves and footpads and prostitutes . . ."

"Prostitutes?" asked Jingee, suddenly alert. "The same women who came come out here aboard their sampans? The girls from the flower houses?"

"Oh, there are many more bad women than those few who have paddled out here tonight. Whampoa has house after house of flower girls. They all have sampans and make life miserable for good, respectable—"

Jingee interrupted, looking at the others. "That's where we could get a boat. A flower house."

Gilbert was instantly critical. "A crazy idea, mister. A crazier and more dangerous idea I have never heard!"

Babcock liked the idea but added, "If it's so dangerous we should have an alternative plan."

"We could divide into two groups," said Kiro. "One group could try to get a boat from a flower girl house. Another group tries somewhere else, like a fishing boat or a vendor."

Despite Cheng-So Gilbert's protestations, the plan for two groups began to take shape.

Groot was the last to climb the bamboo ladder from the hold. Babcock had gone first, carrying a rope and knotting it around a capstan to make an escape route over the starboard side. Jud and Kiro climbed up next and crawled across deck to the gunwale, followed by Jingee and a reluctant Cheng-So Gilbert. Groot watched Jingee urge Gilbert over the side before he himself scrambled out. The voices hummed behind him on the poop deck as he gently replaced the iron grating over the hatch.

Crawling across the deck, he peered down at the sampans bobbing between the three war junks. Beyond, the night's darkness had swallowed the other men swimming to their agreed destinations. He climbed over the side and lowered himself down the rope until he felt the greasy black water envelop his bare feet.

Putting strength into his strokes, Groot swam silently towards the western wharves, too frightened to look back at the war junks. In an attempt to calm himself, he forced his mind back to his boyhood, when he had swum in the canals of Amsterdam, sneaking away from his aunt's house to go swimming with his friends.

Would he ever return to Holland, or save enough money to buy a passage home on a Dutch East Indies merchantman? As he cleaved his way across the harbour, he realised that he had no real reason to go back to Holland. He had no family there now, no friends. His closest friends were the other four Marines and, of course, the *schipper*.

With each stroke, Groot counted the men he had seen killed since Horne had taken them from the prisons of Bombay Castle. The crew aboard Horne's first command, the *Eclipse* . . . The convicts on Bull Island . . . The first Marines: Bapu . . . then Mustafa . . .

The night air felt warm against his dripping body as he pulled himself up to a wooden pile. Clinging to the encrusted wood, he looked around him in the darkness, catching his breath. The *China Flyer* had disappeared from her anchorage across the harbour. The three junks still lay quietly at anchor, giving no sign that the Hoppo's men had discovered their escape. The Merchant's Pier was too far away for Groot to see if Jingee, Kiro and Cheng-So Gilbert had reached their destination.

Summoning his strength, he shinned up the pile and grabbed the edge of the clay-packed pier, cautiously raising his head to see if Babcock and Jud had already arrived.

Two bodies lay face-up in the darkness.

Groot hissed quietly.

Jud raised an arm.

Babcock whispered from his prone position, "Groot, if you start talking now I'll choke you."

Grinning, Groot clambered on to the pier. Why did Babcock always say he talked too much?

The night sky was starry above the three men as they lay on the pier, listening to the waves slapping and the harbour sounds rising all about them—the call of a woman's voice, the plucking of a stringed instrument, the caterwauls of cats.

Jud rolled onto his belly and, feeling the wharf's clay

between his fingertips, suggested, "Rub this on your face and arms, you two. Darken yourselves like me."

As Babcock and Groot followed his advice, he added, "Rub some in your hair, too, Groot. Keep it from shining so white in the night."

Then they crawled along the pier in single file, standing upright only when they reached the shadowy warehouses.

A dog barked inside a flat-roofed building.

Jud listened for men's voices. Satisfied that no one had been alerted by the alarm, he dashed across an alleyway. Peering round the corner, he beckoned Groot and Babcock to follow.

Jumping from shadow to shadow, lane to lane, Jud raised his hand when they reached a narrow lane festooned with dimly-glowing paper lanterns.

"This must be one of those places," he whispered.

Groot and Babcock surveyed the double row of reed-fronted shacks; the street was empty except for a grass hatted man dragging a large bag behind him along the garbage-strewn street.

Jud pointed at the door nearest them. "Is this the house we agreed on?"

"First on the right?" Babcock looked around him. "Has to be it."

Groot smiled at the thought of Cheng-So Gilbert knowing such a place.

"Let me go first," whispered Jud.

"Scare the ladies good and proper," quipped Babcock as he dug into the pocket of his sodden breeches.

Producing a leather pouch, he withdrew three coins, passed one to Jud and, giving the second to Groot, said, "Enjoy yourself, mate."

Taking the coin, Groot thought of the last woman he

had been with in Bombay, how she had driven him from her hut for jabbering too much. Tonight he hoped that he would be able to keep quiet. It was no secret that he talked incessantly when he was nervous . . .

24

Fishermen and Flower Girls

A midnight mist had begun inching across the harbour by the time Jingee, Kiro and Cheng-So Gilbert waded ashore in a swamp beyond the Merchants' Wharf. Anxious to get out of the oily water, Gilbert ran in long, splashing steps, looking for a tree or branch to grip on to for support in the marshy shallows.

"Shhh," cautioned Kiro, motioning Gilbert to stop making so much noise. Before the interpreter had time to explain his actions, Jingee grabbed both him and Kiro by the arms and pulled them down to water-level.

Pointing through reeds, he whispered, "Boat."

The three men knelt chest-deep in the filthy swamp, watching a sampan drift slowly along the edge of the reed beds. A lantern swung from the boat's low prow, one man standing above it with a spear poised high over his shoulder, a second man gently poling the sampan through the water, eyes trained on the light's phosphorescent reflection.

"What are they doing?" whispered Cheng-So Gilbert.

"Octopus," Kiro answered.

"Octopus?" Cheng-So Gilbert looked anxiously around him in the swamp.

"The lantern attracts the octopus to the surface," whispered Kiro, pleased to be the one explaining facts to the Chinese interpreter for a change. "They are drawn to the light and the fisherman stabs them."

Jingee was more interested in the plan to find a boat than in hearing about octopus fishermen. He said, "There are only two of them and three of us. Why don't we tip over the sampan and take it?"

Kiro disagreed. "Even if we could surprise them and take it, another sampan might be following close behind and would rush to their aid."

Determined to seize the fishermen's boat, Jingee moved through the reeds, looking up and down the harbour for approaching craft. To his right, another lantern appeared in the hazy darkness—two men armed with spears instead of one.

Jingee crouched while the second sampan passed and then waded back to Kiro. "We wait longer," he admitted.

Gilbert asked impatiently, "What if they only come in twos and threes? We can't stay here all night."

Kiro remained calm. "Then we swim down the harbour and steal a boat from the wharf."

"Oh, we're certain to get caught," Gilbert moaned. "We'll all be thrown into prison. I'll be beheaded as a traitor."

Irritated by the Chinaman's cowardice, Jingee chided him, "Stop complaining. You knew the risks before we started."

Cheng-So Gilbert was not cowardly; he merely wished he was not here tonight, not involved with the Bombay Marines in a rescue attempt for their leader. He remembered how excited he had been when he had originally been hired by the East India Company to serve traders as an interpreter between Macao and Madras. The Chinese considered Europeans inferior, avoiding their companionship, calling them barbarians and unclean. Being half-caste, Cheng-So Gilbert not only suffered prejudice in China but also found difficulty in obtaining employment. As Englishmen were equally suspicious of the Chinese, they welcomed a man of mixed blood more than someone of pure Chinese descent. Heartened by that acceptance, Gilbert began to entertain hopes of travelling to England and making his fortune in the great capital of London. But what would happen to his dreams if the Manchu found him involved in a covert plan to abduct Adam Horne from an Imperial war junk?

"Look." Kiro pointed out into the bay.

Gilbert and Jingee sloshed forward through the marsh and saw a small junk with a gold dragon fluttering from its mast.

"The imperial flag," gasped Gilbert.

"A patrol boat," said Kiro.

"Do you think they're looking for us?" asked Jingee.

Gilbert was firm. "Now you will cancel these foolish plans."

"Cancel?" Jingee asked indignantly. "How are we to rescue Captain Horne?"

Gilbert took a deep breath, baffled by such stupidity. Surely a man's loyalty was first to himself.

"The women think we're from a Dutch colony on Java," whispered Groot as he, Jud and Babcock followed three Chinese courtesans along a suspended bamboo footbridge to the harbour moorings. Groot had been made the group's spokesman in the women's house when it had become clear that the courtesans had learned Dutch from trading ships visiting Whampoa.

"What reason did you give them for wanting them to row us out to the war junks?" asked Jud, behind him.

"I haven't told them yet where we want to go," Groot

whispered. "I just said we wanted to have a ride in their sampan."

"You better say something soon." Babcock looked at the three giggling women ahead of them on the narrow footbridge.

"There's no reason to worry," insisted Groot. "It's like Cheng-So Gilbert said: flower girls keep sampans to take customers around the harbour."

The three women were short, one more corpulent than the others and one of the slim women considerably older than her two companions. Each carried a bamboo pole from which dangled a paper lantern, and they had also brought earthen bottles of spirits from which they kept pausing to sip, chattering and giggling among themselves as they replaced the stoppers and continued towards the moorings.

"I've never seen women drink so much," Babcock complained as the courtesans took one last swig before descending a bamboo ladder to a cluster of sampans bobbing beneath the bridge.

Groot defended them. "It's the custom in China for women to drink as much as men. Especially at banquets."

"Is this their version of a banquet?" Jud laughed.

"Maybe any visitor means a feast."

Babcock frowned, "Ummm. We'll see."

The women had begun to climb down the ladder, gripping one side while managing to carry their lantern poles and bottles, and to grasp the hems of their long robes.

Jud followed; then Babcock, then Groot, stepping cautiously into the long, narrow boat as it tilted in the water.

Leather curtains hung from the front and back of the sampan's arched central awning. Inside there were colourful cushions and rosewood boxes scattered over the reed matting, and the air was redolent of incense. Two of the women waved to their guests to rest on the cushions while the third—the most corpulent—crawled towards the aft curtain.

"That's your girl, Groot." Babcock elbowed him. "Stick with her."

"Is she rowing?"

"Go and find out."

"Should I row for her?"

Babcock ignored Groot's sudden nerves, becoming increasingly interested in the other two women; one courtesan patted a heap of cushions for him to sit on beside her; the third nodded animatedly to Jud.

Jud returned the woman's smiles and, waving Groot towards the curtain, whispered, "Just keep us on course."

Lingering half-in, half-out of the curtain, Groot asked, "What if she won't go near the war junks?"

"Now's your time to learn how to handle a woman, mate," called Babcock as he sank down on the cushions.

Beads of perspiration coursed through the dried clay on Groot's brow as he left the sweet-smelling cabin.

Inside, Jud settled down on the reed matting, groaning pleasurably as his companion knelt behind his head, rubbing his broad shoulders with her tiny yellow hands and singing a soft song.

Closing his eyes, he admitted, "This is exactly what I need."

"Don't get too comfortable," warned Babcock.

"We've got time for a little relaxation."

Babcock was not listening; his companion had unlocked one of the small rosewood boxes, smiling as she extended it to Babcock, offering him a choice of *dim-sun* pastries with one hand while her other hand stroked his leg.

Outside the cabin, the chubby woman had lit more lanterns, festooning the sampan with coloured paper shades. Seating herself on a thwart, the vessel's single oar seemed unwieldy in her small hands, but she used it deftly, only pausing to take an occasional drink of arrack. Offering the earthen bottle to Groot, she laughed when he refused a drink, and returned to her work.

The harbour traffic had thinned as the night-time mist spread across the water. Groot stood up periodically to make certain they were moving westwards towards the three war junks, then settled down again in front of the curtain, trying to ignore the voices of Jud and Babcock rising behind him.

The small boat was half-way across the harbour, and Groot was peering around the curve of the awning to check the sampan's progress, when he saw a junk approaching through the mist.

Scrambling up, he spotted a flag emblazoned with a gold dragon flapping gently from the mast.

Ducking through the leather curtain, he whispered, "Quick. A patrol boat."

Babcock looked up from his woman. "What?"

"A patrol boat," Groot repeated more loudly, pointing nervously towards the prow.

Behind him, the fat woman had ceased rowing and began calling through the night to the junk.

Babcock and Jud looked quizzically at one another; the two women jumped to their feet, holding out their hands and chattering in Chinese.

"What do they want?" asked Babcock. "We've already paid them."

"More money," answered Jud, looking from one woman to the other.

"What the hell for?"

Behind them, the third woman stuck her head through the curtain, also holding out her hand, shrilling at Groot in pidgin Dutch.

Groot translated. "They need money to pay the patrol boat."

"Pay?" Babcock swung his feet on to the matting. "Pay what?"

"A *cumshaw*. A tax to row their sampan around the harbour at night."

Grudgingly, Babcock dug into his breeches for the leather money pouch.

At the same hour, on the eastern edge of Whampoa harbour, a half-naked man stood on the verandah of a small stilted house. Having been awakened from his sleep by a strange noise, the man gripped a knife in one hand as he peered into the night's misty darkness. Looking over the bamboo railing, he saw two strangers pushing his boat into the water. As he began shouting at them to stop, a figure emerged from the darkness beside him, raised one hand and chopped him across the back of the neck. The attacker hurriedly bound the unconscious man with leather thongs and, taking his knife and a coil of rope, shinned down a pole to the water and began swimming to catch up with the other two men in the stolen boat.

25

The Waterfowl

A pall of dense mist enshrouded the three Imperial war junks anchored within the harbour's western arm. Their deck lanterns shone no brighter than yellow smudges in the night.

Horne turned from the starboard windows of his floating prison, wondering again if Fanshaw had been correct in warning him that he would soon be moved from the junk to a land gaol.

His earlier feeling of frustration had mellowed into a calm composure as he systematically considered the options open to him. After trying the door and inspecting the narrow windows lining both sides of the cabin, he abandoned any hope of immediate escape. Even the wooden louvres beneath the windows would be too noisy to remove from their frames. There might be an opportunity to break away from an escort if he was transferred to a prison on land, but he could not plan for that without knowing the size of his escort, or the method of transport.

Instead, he spent his time going over the defence he would present at the court of inquiry George Fanshaw had said he would have to face. The job would be to

persuade the interrogators that the East India Company
had sent him to Canton to recover the *China Flyer* and
deliver George Fanshaw back to Fort St. George. It
would be his word against Fanshaw's if the written orders
had been destroyed.

Horne's case would be simpler if the Chinese gave his
Marines a chance to testify about the reason for the mission; but were the men still here in Whampoa? If Fanshaw had not been lying about the *Huma* being towed
back down the Pearl River, Babcock, Groot, Jingee, Jud
and Kiro might have rejoined the crew before the ship
returned to Macao and the opium depot on Kam-Sing-
Moon.

A sound disturbed his thoughts.

Lying motionless on his pallet, he stared blankly at the
oil lamp flickering beside his pallet as he listened to the
soft warble of a bird.

Why did the call sound so familiar? Where had he
heard it before? Bombay? Years ago in England?

The gentle cooing sounded a second time, unobtrusive
yet definitely unique.

Bird calls? What do they mean to me? What association do I have with that call and . . .

The soft tremolo came a third time.

Horne remembered.

It was the same call Cheng-So Gilbert had imitated in
his first days out of Madras—the sound of the Whampoa
waterfowls that were so delicious to eat.

Swinging his bare feet to the deck, Horne moved to
the starboard windows and looked down at the courtesans' sampans bobbing gently below him. Through the
mist, he saw that one sampan had drifted closer to the
junk than the others, and that a fat-faced girl was looking
up at him.

Was she a late-comer hoping to join the guards' party

on the poop-deck? Or had she purposely been left aboard the sampan by her friends? Or was it possible that . . .

The waterfowl's warble came again. Horne moved to look out of the other side of the cabin. There was a face pressed against the panes, and he came to a stop in the middle of the cabin.

Jingee! Hanging by a . . . rope?

Crossing the cabin in three strides, Horne blew out the lantern beside the bed and fell to his knees. He crawled towards the junk's larboard windows and pressed his mouth against the low louvres, whispering, "What are you doing here?"

Jingee's voice came to him through the slats. "We came to rescue you, Captain sahib."

"How did you get here?"

"We swam ashore and stole boats, Captain sahib."

"Where have the Chinese been keeping you?"

"On the next junk, Captain sahib. Earlier today we saw an Englishman row out to this ship. That's how we guessed you were here."

"That was Fanshaw."

"So we guessed, Captain sahib."

"Did you all escape?"

"In two groups, Captain sahib."

"Who's here with you?"

"Kiro and the Chinaman are with me, Captain sahib. Babcock, Groot and Jud are below in a sampan from a flower house on shore."

Horne remembered the fat-faced courtesan looking up at his cabin.

"Are you armed?" he asked.

"Kiro and I have knives."

Horne explained, "I tried opening the windows and removing these louvres, but I can't do it without creating a disturbance."

"I saw you have one guard outside your door, Captain sahib. Are there others?"

"Yes, but they're merrymaking with the women. My guard goes and returns. I hear his footsteps."

"Shall I ambush him, Captain sahib?"

"Where's Kiro?"

"Knotting a rope to the starboard side. To escape to the sampan."

"Cheng-So Gilbert?"

"Rowing our little boat round to the sampan."

"Do we know if the women are trustworthy?"

"Two have drunk themselves into unconsciousness, Captain sahib. The fat one's ready to pass out."

Horne weighed the preparations his men had made—boats, rope, knives. Realising that the escape must be quick and kept as simple as possible, he explained to Jingee how they should proceed.

Horne tapped lightly on the cabin door. He did not want to arouse the revellers on the poop-deck, but at the same time he had to attract the guard's attention.

Rapping louder, he paused when he heard footsteps approaching the iron-banded door. Listening more closely he could hear only distant raucous laughter, the giggling of women, the sound of a stringed instrument enlivening the midnight party.

He knocked a third time, venturing in English, "Please, I must speak to you."

As a key sounded in the lock, he prepared an excuse for having the door opened in case Jingee had not reached the agreed spot. The metallic scratch of the key stopped abruptly and, outside the door, he heard a thud.

There was another silence and then the key sounded again in the lock.

Horne stood back from the door as it opened a few

inches. He pushed it wider and stepping out of the cabin, spotted the guard slumped on the deck. No one else was in sight. Pulling the guard into the cabin, he shoved him on to the pallet, pulled the blanket over him and crept back to the door.

From the protection of the shadows, he saw the revellers gathered round the glow of their lanterns and charcoal braziers on the poop-deck. Satisfied that he was temporarily unobserved, he hoisted himself on to the cabin roof and, finding the rope knotted there by Kiro, dropped over the starboard side, lowering himself hand-over-hand to the water. Then he released the rope and swam silently towards the sampan.

The boat was sitting low in the water, and Horne pulled himself cautiously aboard, wary of the sampan capsizing under the heavy passenger load.

As soon as Horne rolled aboard, the boat began moving. The chubby courtesan sat propped against the stern but was too inebriated to paddle. As she smiled blankly into the night, Jud and Kiro lay flat on both sides, paddling from prone positions with oars taken from the fisherman's boat they were towing.

Satisfied with their progress, Horne crawled to the curtained awning, the stench of alcohol assailing his nostrils as he entered. Babcock, Groot and Jingee were there, waiting anxiously between the unconscious bodies of two painted courtesans, loud snores emerging from the women's gaping mouths.

26

Down River

The morning light was breaking over the pine-covered hills as Horne moved down the Pearl River with his men and Cheng-So Gilbert. Two hours had passed since they had abandoned the courtesans, bound and gagged, under a willow tree and stripped their sampan of its decorative lanterns and cushions. They had continued down river, travelling in two groups to avoid attracting unnecessary attention to themselves on their way to Macao.

Horne went with Jud, Groot and Cheng-So Gilbert in the sampan. Babcock, Kiro and Jingee kept to the reeds on the opposite bank, paddling the fisherman's boat. Both groups wore oddments of clothing they had stolen from washing lines in fishing villages along the way.

A ragged piece of homespun hung from Horne's head to his shoulders as he poled the sampan through the eddying shallows, eyes alert as Groot and Gilbert sat watchful near the prow.

River traffic had been sparse throughout the dark morning hours. Every owl's hoot and crane's flutter had tried the men's nerves, but the only travellers they had seen were two sampans moving in the opposite direction.

The peasants showed little interest in Horne's men; they likewise pretended to be undisturbed by them. The journey continued southwards, slow and monotonous, the two groups periodically emerging from the reeds, waving a brown rag to signal they were maintaining their progress.

After sunrise, when Groot was due to take over the pole, Horne heard a noise behind him. Glancing over his shoulder he saw a mast above the distant rushes.

Whistling, he waved Groot to his knees.

Groot spotted the tall mast rounding the bend, but Cheng-So Gilbert had not yet seen it.

When he eventually caught sight of the approaching vessel, he gasped, "The Imperial flag."

Horne had already identified the official Manchu dragon; he beckoned Gilbert to him, ordering, "Take the pole instead of Groot."

"Where are you going?" asked Gilbert.

Horne waved for Groot, answering, "Inside."

The vessel was rapidly gaining distance on the far side of the river. Horne observed their progress through the leather curtain, guessing, "They could be looking for us."

"Do you think Babcock's seen it?" asked Groot beside him.

Horne was concerned about the same thing. It was time for the other men to signal from the reeds and, if they had not spotted the patrol boat, they would emerge directly in front of it.

"Gilbert, call to them," ordered Horne through the curtain.

"To Mr. Babcock?"

"To the patrol."

"Call what?"

"Anything. But shout loud enough to alert the others that somebody's nearby. Quick."

"What if they come and search us?" asked Gilbert.

"We have to risk that," Horne said. "Remember you're a fisherman. Don't sound too educated."

Horne, Groot and Jud lay motionless inside the curved cabin, careful not to rock the sampan as Cheng-So Gilbert poled his way out through the reeds.

"He's going to give us away," whispered Groot.

"Let's just hope he doesn't capsize the boat."

"Or get caught in the river's main current," added Jud.

"Or drop the pole."

Outside the cabin, Gilbert had begun calling to the patrol, his voice quavering with nerves.

"Louder," Horne urged through the curtain.

Groot whispered, "What do you think he's saying."

They fell silent as a reply came back across the river. They exchanged glances, listening, expecting the patrol to cross the swift-moving current . . .

But nothing.

"You can come out now," whispered Gilbert.

Horne peered through the leather curtain. The patrol was moving down river. Across the wide body of water, a brown cloth waved from the reeds—all was clear.

"What did you say to get rid of them so quickly, Mr. Gilbert?" Horne asked, crawling from the cabin.

"I called out that my poor wife and eight children had lost all control of their bowels. I asked the patrol boat if they would take them down river to Macao. I said that only my grandmother knows how to stop the crying woman and sick babies from making such an awful mess."

"What made you think of that?"

Gilbert sheepishly dropped his eyes. "Because I was about to do that very thing myself, Captain Horne."

• • •

The men were tired and ravenously hungry by the time they reached Macao the next day. They had moored four times since leaving Whampoa, stopping to sleep when the river traffic was at its height, and to share the small bits of fish and curd Cheng-So Gilbert had managed to buy from a passing sampan.

Activity was at its busiest in Macao during the morning, barges and junks and small reed coracles moving to and fro past the twin forts that guarded the harbour entrance. But there was no sign of the *Huma* or the *China Flyer* at anchorage within the harbour. Horne conceded that Fanshaw had not been lying to him, that the *Huma* had been taken to Kam-Sing-Moon for the chests of opium to be unloaded at the government's depot.

Groot said, "I bet the *China Flyer*'s also been taken to that island. She must have had cargo when we saw her in Whampoa. She sat low in the water, *schipper*."

"We'll soon find out." Horne looked at the men, asking, "Are you willing to try slipping past those two forts out there?"

"We made it this far," said Babcock, pulling on his big ear.

"What other choice do we have, Captain Sahib?"

"None, Jingee. That's our one way to the sea and Kam-Sing-Moon."

Cheng-So Gilbert, bolstered by his success in fending off the patrol boat and securing food for the men, bragged, "Why would they stop us? We're only lowly fishermen. Let *me* get us through!"

The men exchanged glances. Did pride truly go before a fall?

27

Kam-Sing-Moon

The sun shone dully on the slate hillside forming the conical island of Kam-Sing-Moon. Porters moved back and forth, carrying bow-topped chests from the *China Flyer* at the end of the wharf to the warehouse at the foot of the barren mountain.

When the porters had concluded their task, Lothar Schiller greeted their supervisor at the port entry and accepted the receipt for Fanshaw's *cumshaw* of opium.

"I assume that clears me to leave," said Schiller in German, knowing no Chinese to speak to the depot official.

The supervisor bowed his head with its cylindrical blue cap, replying in Chinese as he gestured towards the *Huma* anchored across the natural harbour. Schiller understood that the man wanted him to move alongside the Bombay Marine frigate.

Watching the official turn on the gangplank and stride back up the wharf to the warehouse, Schiller thought of Fanshaw's instructions: the *China Flyer* was to remain here at Kam-Sing-Moon until Fanshaw arrived from Whampoa.

What if he were to abandon Fanshaw and leave China without him?

Schiller doubted if the depot officials could detain him here. Within the last hour, the island guard had come to the end of their watch and, at the moment, only two cumbersome junks lay in the harbour, obviously waiting for the next watch to arrive.

But, then, did the Chinese even care what Schiller did now that they had taken what they wanted from the hold?

The Co-Hung, too, might be detaining Fanshaw in Canton, forbidding him to rejoin his captain and crew. Fanshaw had worried about such an event.

Schiller mounted the quarter-deck, weighing the possibility of striking out from Chinese waters against the alternative of waiting here for Fanshaw and the gold owing to him and the crew.

But had not Fanshaw reneged on his promises before? He had not paid the men on their arrival in Whampoa, nor, before that, when they had reached Macao. And what about when he had bribed the men to fire on the helpless Sulu islanders and then failed to honour his promise?

Fanshaw was planning to sail to London. Schiller had learnt that much from him. He suspected that Fanshaw would next promise to pay them when they reached England.

Schiller would like to go back to England . . . but how badly?

To bring a ship from the Orient represented a major feat for any seaman. He could find a good job in London with such credentials.

Contemplating the arduous voyage down the South China Sea, across the Indian Ocean, and up the west coast of Africa to Europe, he worried about the condition of the *China Flyer*. At least a month of repairs was necessary—no, vital. Fanshaw had less respect for the *China Flyer* than he did for the crew. Schiller doubted if they could sail as far as Africa's Cape without trouble.

The alternative was Madras.

Should he risk returning to Madras and learning whether the East India Company had put a price on his head for being an accomplice with George Fanshaw?

As Schiller crossed his quarter-deck, his attention focused on the *Huma*. Seeing activity in the shrouds of the Marine frigate, he wondered if she was preparing to weigh anchor.

Horne and his men lay in a line along Kam-Sing-Moon's jagged crest, looking down at the Chinese porters unloading wooden chests from the *China Flyer* and carrying them to the warehouse at the head of the pier, like ants burdened with breadcrumbs.

Jingee lay next to Horne above the crescent-shaped harbour. He pointed down to the grey-tiled warehouse, whispering, "That must be the opium depot, Captain sahib."

Groot observed from the other side of Horne, "Those chests must be Fanshaw's gift to the Hoppo."

Jingee added, "I wonder if Fanshaw's come down river yet from Canton."

Horne's interest was focused on the *Huma*, observing that the sails were furled but the anchor not dropped. The Chinese must believe taut cables held the ship more effectively in its anchorage.

Jud spotted activity on deck. "The crew's still aboard, sir."

Horne had also seen the brown-skinned sailors and was greatly relieved.

"How many guards do you think are posted with our men?" asked Kiro on the far side of Groot.

The distance between the summit and harbour was too great for Horne to see men's features or clothing. He longed for his spyglass.

"Men, we shall follow separate paths down the slope," he said finally, after studying the two ships and the pair of junks anchored beyond.

He pointed to the *Huma*. "Jingee and Kiro, do you see those shore cables?"

They saw the black lines stretching from the larboard side to the rocky shoreline.

Horne swept his finger to the right of the mountainside. "You follow the gully down . . . there. Wait behind that boulder for me to give you a signal. Then start climbing the aft cables."

He continued to the others. "You three keep to the ridge. Run along the right ledge. Come out down there by the . . . prow. See?"

Babcock, Groot and Jud followed the direction of Horne's finger, nodding as they understood the route to the southern promontory.

Horne concluded, "Mr. Gilbert, you stay behind with me."

Gilbert's excitement was growing, his confidence swollen by his success in guiding the Marines safely past the twin forts at the entrance to Macao harbour.

"What do you want me to do this time, Captain Horne?" he asked, feeling like a Bombay Marine himself.

"I'll tell you when the time comes, Mr. Gilbert."

Horne looked back at Kiro and Jingee. "Remember, wait for my signal."

"Aye, aye, sir," answered Kiro.

Horne glanced once more from the junks to the pier, to the warehouse, before ordering, "Now . . . go!"

Kiro led the way, followed by Jingee bent forward in a crouch. A few moments later Babcock, Groot and Jud

disappeared in the opposite direction. Horne watched the
five men darting from cover to cover, creeping down the
mountainside. Then he beckoned to Cheng-So Gilbert to
follow him.

He went slowly, periodically cautioning Gilbert not to
move too quickly and create a landslide. The sun was
high and the wind off the open sea did little to cool the
heat reflected from the slate mountainside. As Horne
crept cautiously downwards, his eyes darted from the
Huma to the porters still moving along the wharf with
the opium chests, to the two junks now directly below
him in the cove.

Reaching the foot of the incline, he checked to see that
the Marines were all in place before he whispered to
Gilbert, "Now. Get ready to call."

"Call?"

"To the guards aboard the *Huma*."

"Chinese guards?" Cheng-So Gilbert looked alarmed,
his new-found confidence disappearing. "But, Captain, I
don't know what dialect they speak, what to say . . ."
Trembling, he mopped the perspiration from his brow.

"Use a court dialect," Horne instructed him. "Demand
to speak to their commander-in-chief. Be forceful."

Gilbert glanced nervously round the harbour. "Won't . . .
they hear me?" He nodded at the porters still trudging
between the warehouse and the *China Flyer*.

"Not if you don't scream at the top of your lungs."

Not waiting for Gilbert to protest further, Horne
pushed him from the protection of the rock.

As the Chinaman splashed into the shallow cove, hail-
ing the *Huma* in Chinese, Horne signalled to Jingee and
Kiro to make their move.

Aboard ship, the crew ran to the rail with three guards
when they heard Gilbert's voice. Recognising the chubby
Chinese interpreter standing knee-deep in the lapping wa-

ter, they looked beyond him and saw Horne, and they quickly overpowered the guards.

By then, the Marines had already begun climbing the far cables.

28

Clear for Action

The crowd of nut-brown faces gathered round Horne near
the forecastle, beaming with pleasure at the sight of their
captain. Excitedly, they began patting one another, laughing and exchanging warm hugs, certain they were on
their way home.

Horne waved the crew into silence, explaining in a low
but firm voice, "We don't leave China without finishing
our job here."

Jubilant smiles froze on the crew's faces.

"We came to China to find the *China Flyer*. Now that
we've found her—" He pointed across the harbour.
"—we must take her and lead her back to Madras."

The men looked apprehensively at one another.

"Are you willing to fight?" asked Horne.

Cautious nods.

"Do you want to share in a reward for bringing a Company ship back to Fort St. George?"

Deeper, more earnest nods.

"Then seize the *China Flyer* and I promise you your
pay will be doubled on your return to Madras."

Cheers deafened Horne.

Silencing the crew, he cautioned in a voice barely louder than a whisper, "You must work quickly and quietly, and make every movement count.

"And I want you to be ready for a fight. Not only from the ship's crew, but the Chinese also could join in the battle. There are two junks out there and cannon on shore. But if we set to work immediately and work quickly, we can do it.

"Remember how we broke out from the escort of Sulu pirates, how quickly you worked and followed orders?"

The men grinned, enthusiasm growing among them.

Lowering his voice to a whisper, he asked, "Can you work that quickly and quietly again?"

The men were beginning to jig with nervous anticipation, nodding their heads in answer to Horne's question.

"Good. This is what we'll do and how we'll do it."

Appointing each of his Marines to their usual crewmen, Horne gave them their instructions and sent them to their stations. Then he hurried to his cabin to retrieve his spyglass from his desk. Looking round the familiar quarters, it seemed years and not mere days since he had been abducted from his sleep.

Hearing the patter of bare feet overhead, he told himself not to waste precious moments and turned to go back to the quarter-deck. Here Jud was already leading the men aloft to the yards; below him Kiro's gun crews were at their stations; Jingee was forming his gang into water and sand brigades; Groot stood at the wheel.

Satisfied that every man understood his instructions, Horne signalled to Babcock and the taut shore cables were severed in a series of sharp axe blows.

The drift of the tide caught the frigate in an instant. Feeling the tug, Horne signalled Jud, and the canvas thundered from the yards. The ship shuddered; the decks groaned; and, suddenly, the foretopsail filled with the wind.

Horne no longer guarded his voice. "Man the braces!"

"Aye, aye, sir."

"Lay her on larboard tack."

"Aye, aye, *schipper*."

"Set a course—first—towards the mouth of the cove."

At the wheel Groot grinned, his face washed, peasant rags gone, his dark cap set back on his sun-bright hair.

Blocks chattered as the *Huma* paid off in the wind, sweeping away from her anchorage.

Eyeglass in hand, Horne studied the activity aboard the two Chinese junks as the *Huma* sped towards them in the instant grab of the wind. He was pleased with his decision to avoid contact with the junks. Why risk war with the Chinese? His orders were to regain Company property; that and that alone must be his goal.

Watching the prow sweep from the war junks to the wharf, he wondered who controlled the frigate. The Chinese had finished unloading the opium chests, but where was George Fanshaw? Was he aboard with Lothar Schiller or still in Canton?

Knowing he had little time to waste on speculation, Horne remembered his plan and, as the ship heeled towards the *China Flyer*, he cupped both hands to his mouth, calling, "Prepare for action."

Cheers greeted the command; Horne beamed. He had returned home.

Lothar Schiller's first thought on seeing activity aboard the *Huma* was that the Chinese were moving the Marine ship from her anchorage. But observing the canvas spread like a great white flower unfolding in warm sunlight, and spotting the gun ports open in rapid succession to reveal a row of threatening black holes, he wondered if the ship's crew might have rebelled against their Chinese captors—or gone crazy.

What was happening across the harbour? Was the *Huma* preparing to make way for open waters?

Seeing the sails catch the wind, he gaped in astonishment as the *Huma* changed course and, making her stays, swept towards the two Chinese junks anchored near the mouth of the harbour. Pure madness! How could they hope to attack the two junks and escape? Did they not realise that a relief watch would soon be arriving from Macao?

Schiller watched the ship continue in a wide arc, realising with horror that the *Huma* was heading—*Gott in Himmel*—not for the junks but for the wharf, towards the *China Flyer*!

"Raise anchor!" he shouted to the crew.

Schiller's men remained inert on deck, staring transfixed at the ship's manoeuvres in the mouth of the cove.

"Raise anchor, you damned buggers!" roared Schiller with uncharacteristic impatience.

A boom aboard the *Huma* attracted the men's attention; a puff of blue smoke from the nearing gun ports hurried them into action.

"Hands aloft," ordered Schiller, shouting louder. *"Prepare for action!"*

As the seamen hurried into the shrouds, chains ground through the hawse-hole and Schiller pulled open his spyglass to concentrate again on the *Huma*. No further smoke rose from the gun ports. The first explosion must have been a ranging shot. But for whom?

Dropping the spyglass, he studied the action closer at hand. On the wharf the Chinese porters were scurrying towards the warehouse while troops poured out, surrounding the cannon barricade at the foot of the slate mountain.

"Anchor aweigh, Captain Schiller," came a call amid the ship's confusion.

Schiller had already felt the drift of the ship. Raising his eyes aloft, he saw the canvas dropping, hardening with wind, but, still, he was not satisfied with the speed of the seamen preparing to make way.

"Lay her on starboard tack," he called to his Javanese sailing master, Looie.

"Aye, aye, Captain," came the response from the wiry seaman.

Beyond the jib-boom, he could see that the *Huma* had changed tack again, making way towards the rear of the harbour, heading for the warehouse and the cannon barricade.

What were those crazy devils intending to do? Smash the Chinese depot?

The Chinese evidently feared the same thing, Schiller decided as he heard the shore cannon boom.

At the moment when the Chinese shot splashed short of its target, the *Huma* swung towards the depot's long pier. Schiller instantly saw that he would have no choice but to head for the sea. The *Huma* wanted the *China Flyer*.

In Whampoa, the Co-Hung's chief mandarin, Abutai, sat in his rosewood armchair to receive George Fanshaw in the late afternoon audience at the Co-Hung's headquarters.

Abutai explained in his carefully enunciated Chinese, "We have considered your proposal carefully, Mr. Fanshaw, and have decided not to expand our trade commitment to include a second company from England. It is the Imperial opinion that enough European merchants have access to China."

The rejection stunned Fanshaw. As his mind groped

for words, he sputtered, "But . . . but . . . but a second English company would lower the prices you pay . . . would
destroy the monopoly which the East India Company has
with China . . . will make . . . will make . . ."

Abutai remained steadfast. "I have told you the Co-
Hung's decision, Mr. Fanshaw."

"But you were ready to accept my proposal, great Abutai. To welcome a new company in trade."

"The Co-Hung considers, Mr. Fanshaw. But the
Imperial throne makes the decision. You have heard their
word."

"You accepted my *cumshaw*," Fanshaw argued. "My
gift of opium."

"Do Englishmen expect gifts to be returned when they
do not get their wishes, Mr. Fanshaw?"

"Of course not. I do not mean that."

"You must consider your gift as a humble recognition
for the honour to sail into Chinese waters."

"What about my arrangement with my colleagues in
England?"

"Do you travel half-way around the world, Mr. Fanshaw," Abutai asked arrogantly, "to ask my advice on
your private arrangements at home?"

"No, of course not. But what about the East India
Company? I can hardly go back to Madras—"

Fanshaw stopped. He had taken precautions against a
disappointment such as this. Remembering his foresight
in sending Lothar Schiller down to Kam-Sing-Moon, he
saw that he had to get out of this audience and away
from Whampoa as quickly as possible.

Summoning all the fawning Chinese etiquette he could
muster, he bowed low, saying, "You must accept my
cumshaw of opium as a modest token of esteem to Manchu greatness. I can only hope to return to Canton in the

near future with another proposal to present to your esteemed eminence, lofty Abutai."

The Mandarin was not ready for Fanshaw to leave the chamber. "You again mention the matter of opium, Mr. Fanshaw. In our last meeting, you also spoke of opium. You explained to me that you know of small merchants who are enjoying an illicit traffic in opium along China's coast."

Alerted by the mandarin's words, Fanshaw stuttered, "Sir . . . great Abutai . . . do not think I would deal with such men . . ."

Abutai raised his hand for silence. "The Co-Hung is concerned that too many foreigners might know about such an illegal trade."

"You have my word, sir, that I shall not tell others."

"The Co-Hung needs more than your word, Mr. Fanshaw."

"More?" Fanshaw's head beaded with nervous perspiration. "What do you mean?"

Guards had appeared from behind gilt screens, flanking Fanshaw, their hands on the hilts of their curved swords.

"You are to be held in Canton, Mr. Fanshaw."

"Held?"

"Your presence here will also assuage our displeasure over the disappearance of the Bombay Marines from Imperial custody."

"Adam Horne's disappearance?" Fanshaw did not understand.

Abutai explained, "Captain Horne and his men escaped two nights ago. The anger which the Imperial throne would feel over their disappearance will be softened when they know that another Company man has replaced Adam Horne in prison."

"But I have nothing to do with Horne and his Bombay Marines," Fanshaw shouted, looking from the Mandarin to the guards. "The Company will admit as much!"

"The Co-Hung indeed intends to inform the East India Company of our decision to hold you, sir." He motioned the guards to seize Fanshaw.

"But I have men and a ship waiting for me. My command."

"Your ship will be sent back to Fort St. George with word that we are detaining you in Canton for an indefinite period of time."

"But I have nothing to do with the East India Company. Nothing." Fanshaw was screaming.

Abutai rose from the chair, ignoring Fanshaw's cries.

Trying to break loose from the guards' grip, Fanshaw shouted, "You've been using me. That's what you've been doing. You've been using me to learn what I know about illegal trade going on here. You've been *using me!*"

Abutai departed from the chamber, his robes creating the slightest rustle of silk.

29

The Third Choice

The first strike from the *Huma*'s cannon persuaded Schiller that he must not hesitate in returning fire. After a slow start, the *China Flyer* had weighed anchor and thankfully paid off, her topsails catching the strong breeze off the island. As she gathered way towards the open sea, the bows met the first rollers, spray bursting into feathery silver fans.

On the island the cannon continued firing, but Schiller saw that the *Huma* was well out of the battery's range. He did not understand, though, why the reed-sailed junks across the harbour had made no attempt to intercept the Marine frigate since she had broken from her shore cables. Did they consider themselves inferior in fire-power or manoeuvrability?

Moving his spyglass from the Chinese junks, Schiller again studied the *Huma*, in relentless pursuit of the *China Flyer*, bearing down on her stern. Who was in command of the Marine Frigate? He thought he detected one or two European seamen among the Asian crew. Had the Chinese released Adam Horne from prison? But only an escapee would have to sneak aboard his own ship and break from shore cables.

The idea of not knowing who was giving him chase amused Schiller. Whoever they were, he would give them a good run.

If the wind held, he gauged that he would soon be free of Kam-Sing-Moon. Then he could tack and enjoy the advantage to return gun-fire.

The anticipation of battle excited him, and the gathering speed was tonic to the dejection he had felt since the very beginning of this voyage. Nevertheless, deep within him was a nagging anxiety.

The East India Company wanted George Fanshaw for stealing gold from Fort St. George and commandeering the *China Flyer* from the Madras Roads. Schiller believed that Fanshaw should indeed be apprehended for these crimes—and more. Apart from being a thief and a liar, he was a murderer.

Should he, Schiller, remain loyal to such a man?

Where was Fanshaw? He had ordered Schiller to Kam-Sing-Moon to be ready to escape if the Chinese turned against him. Was he on his way down river at this very moment?

If Fanshaw fell into disfavour with the Chinese, where could he go? The East India Company would arrest him if he returned to Fort St. George; without Chinese support, there would be no new trading company welcoming him back to England. There might also be a price on his head there, sponsored by the East India Company.

Feeling the deck rise and fall beneath his boots, Schiller asked himself if he wanted to be on the run for the rest of his days with the likes of a man such as George Fanshaw, in command of a stolen ship. Would it be better to face the British authorities at this juncture, tell his honest version of the story and take the punishment owing to him for partaking in Fanshaw's unlawful venture?

A cry aloft cut through the sigh of the rigging.

"Sail ho . . . sails to the west . . ."

Schiller raised his spyglass and saw eight spine-sailed junks moving out from Macao—the replacement for the Kam-Sing-Moon watch.

Astern, the *Huma* bore down on him.

Schiller reviewed his choices.

If the *China Flyer* proceeded west, she would sail directly into the Chinese who would undoubtedly return him to the protective custody of Macao. He might never again be able to leave China, or at least, would have to remain here longer than he wished.

The second choice would be to lead the *Huma* farther to sea and engage her in battle until one of them was destroyed.

The third choice was tempting, but was it sensible? The best for his future? Too much of a risk? He would be gambling on the kind of man the *Huma*'s captain was—if indeed it was the Bombay Marine in command of the *Huma*. There was no way of gauging his character with nothing but giant rollers crashing between them.

Remembering that he had taken chances all his life, Schiller decided to risk the third choice: he would show his open gun ports to the Marines and see how quick they would be to fire.

"Are we going to chase Fanshaw all the way back to India?" Babcock stood at his post near Horne on the quarter-deck.

"We don't know if it's Fanshaw."

"Who's in command?"

"I would guess the German, Lothar Schiller. Fanshaw's probably still up river in Whampoa."

"What you got in mind?"·

"The question, Babcock, is what Mr. Schiller has in mind, if indeed that is whom we are pursuing."

As the main topsail cracked in a strong gust pushing off the island, Jud hailed above the cry of the rigging.

Horne snapped open his spyglass and studied the western horizon. "Manchu war junks."

He looked back at the *China Flyer* beyond the harbour mouth.

"Is the German turning to the Chinese for help?" asked Babcock.

Horne steadied the glass to his eye. "No sign yet that he is."

"Are the Chinese going to follow him?"

Horne looked back to the war junks. "No. So far they're keeping formation. They're awkward in the open sea with European ships, and they know it."

"So what do we do, Horne? Get set for a long chase?" asked Babcock.

Horne did not reply; he was studying the *China Flyer* changing course.

"She's going to try to go about—" he began and stopped.

"What's the matter?" asked Babcock, turning to Horne.

"She's opened her gun-ports."

"Now's your chance to blast away," goaded Babcock.

Horne hesitated. Why had the German not tried a ranging shot?

"What are you waiting for?" asked Babcock. "You've got it clear and wide."

Horne studied the distant frigate. The ports were open but no guns were run out. What was Schiller doing?

"What you waiting for?" Babcock asked a second time.

Horne could not explain how he felt. The open gun ports might be a sign, some kind of invitation or test: Schiller might want to see whether the *Huma* would rush an attack or hesitate. If the *Huma* held back, Schiller would know that fair treatment awaited him and his crew if he surrendered . . .

Seeing a flutter aboard the distant ship, Horne raised his spyglass to verify his suspicion. Smiling, he saw that, yes, a white flag of truce was being run up as the *China Flyer* changed course yet again to sail south from Kam-Sing-Moon.

30

The New Marine

Mrs. Watson cornered her husband at their Saturday evening party for her niece and warned, "Don't you dare speak to Captain Horne tonight about Company matters. Allow him time to talk to Emily."

Commodore Watson seemed uncomfortable with the guests milling through Rose Cottage's small parlour and out onto the verandah overlooking the garden. Mopping his damp forehead with a linen handkerchief, he answered, "A man like Adam Horne has little to talk about but duty, my dear."

"You mean you're the one who prefers talking Company business," disagreed Mrs. Watson. The diminutive woman worried that the social gathering might unduly tax her husband's strength. Four months had passed since his worrying illness, but he still had not totally recovered from his faintness and palpitations.

Gulping a cup of fruit punch, Watson smacked his lips, assuring his wife, "Company matters must take some precedence. I've yet to hear details about Horne's mission to China. I know only that Governor Pigot awarded him and his crew the prize money for bringing the *China*

Flyer back to Madras. Pigot writes that Horne's quite a hero now around Fort St. George. The Company's finally starting to recognise him as something other than a down-at-the-heel buccaneer."

"I'm certain Captain Horne deserves all the approbation he receives. You can hear everything from him tomorrow at Bombay Castle. Tonight let the good captain and his men enjoy themselves. I was fearful I might have to postpone the party yet another week." She glanced approvingly across the room at Horne talking to Emily Harkness in a far corner. "I did so want those two young people to meet."

Watson looked from Horne and his wife's niece to the other guests crowding the parlour, mostly East India Company employees and their wives, with a few military and church figures intermixed in the Saturday soirée.

"Too many people in this room," he complained, taking a longer sip of the brightly coloured fruit cup.

The sight of her husband enjoying the pink punch made Mrs. Watson wonder if he had laced her family recipe with gin. Seeing the perspiration beading his forehead, she suggested, "Why don't you go outside into the fresh air, my dear? Talk to the nice young men Captain Horne brought with him to the party."

"A sorry lot those five men are."

"Don't scold. When Captain Horne said he didn't want to abandon his men on their first night in Bombay I insisted he bring them with him this evening."

She lowered her voice. "There are more than five men. Captain Horne brought *seven* guests with him. There's that tall German gentleman, Mr. Schiller, and that short, roly-poly Chinese interpreter, Mr. Gilbert."

Raising her fan, she explained *sotto voce*, "I understand, too, from your secretary, dear, that one of those two men is a candidate for the Bombay Marine—"

Mrs. Watson stopped. She snapped shut her lace fan, her liquid blue eyes dancing with sudden amusement. "How dreadful I am!" she exclaimed. "Listen to me! I scold you about discussing Company affairs at Emily's party and here I am talking about—" She popped open the fan. "—the Bombay Marine."

"Why not? You're bound to have a little salt water in your veins after all these years."

"And perfectly lovely years they've been, too," she replied affectionately. "I wouldn't trade them for any others."

Watson pretended not to notice his wife's sentimental remark. Instead, he raised his big head, eyelids half-lowered, and surveyed the crowded parlour, taking a longer, more fortifying gulp of the rose-red cup.

The air was cooler on the verandah but Groot and Babcock were as uncomfortable there as they had been inside the parlour of Rose Cottage.

"I should have said no to this party," Babcock complained.

"It's good to mix with people," disagreed Groot. "A man too much at sea starts forgetting he belongs to the human race."

"These fancy people have nothing to do with me." Babcock glanced sideways at a short woman hanging on the arm of a vicar, listening solicitously to his every word. "I have more fun talking to Monkey."

The mention of Babcock's pet monkey reminded Groot of a matter he had yet to resolve with the American. "There's something I wanted to mention to you, Babcock. Don't get angry . . . but . . . well . . ."

"Stop beating about the bush. What is it?"

"Sleeping. Every night you . . . well . . . your monkey . . ."

Babcock turned, his eyes narrowing as he demanded, "What about Monkey?"

"He keeps me awake and—"

"Hell, Groot, we've been away for four months. You haven't been near Monkey."

"That's the other problem," Groot hedged.

"What other problem?"

"You . . . you talk in your sleep, Babcock."

"I do?" He pulled his red ear. "What do I say?"

"It's not so much 'say' as . . . shout . . . or yell . . ."

Babcock's aggression continued to wane. "I . . . do?"

"You do. I was wondering if there's something troubling you."

Lowering his voice, Babcock looked guardedly around him, asking, "What do I yell, Groot? Is it, you know, very . . . personal?"

"It's about your Pa."

"I talk about my old man?"

Groot nodded. "Yah. You tell him not to hit you. Every night you shout out, 'Don't hit me, Pa . . . Don't hit me.'"

Babcock's face blanched. He remembered his nightmares about fighting with his father, how his father turned into Horne in the dreams, how he was unable to hit Horne, calling him "Pa."

His head down, he mumbled, "Don't mention this to nobody, Groot. I'd appreciate that."

"No, of course not," Groot quickly assured him.

Pulling on his ear, Babcock drawled, "As for Monkey keeping you awake, well, I've been thinking about making a little outside cage for him anyway . . . at least for nights . . . the pesky devil's been bothering me, too . . ."

He looked beseechingly at Groot. "Please don't mention nothing to nobody? About me calling out to Pa."

• • •

Jud and Kiro were standing at the other end of the verandah, cowering in the shadows made by the paper lanterns strung along the overhanging eaves. Jud noticed the
blank smile on Kiro's face and asked, "What are you
thinking about, my friend? You look as if you are a thousand miles away from here."

"Friends. Families." Kiro's shrug was lifeless, unlike
his usual aggressiveness on the gun-deck.

"Are you missing yours?"

"I never had a family."

"Do you think you ever will?" asked Jud, remembering
how he took his own wife and son everywhere with
him—in the breeze, in his songs, inside his head.

Kiro considered the question. "The friends I have take
the place of family. Horne and all you."

Jud grinned. "I think we're going to get one more
brother, and very soon."

Kiro's attentiveness returned. "Do you really think
Horne's going to make him a Marine?"

They turned and looked at the new candidate through
the parlour window.

Jingee moved impatiently from one foot to the other beside Cheng-So Gilbert who was talking to the small
group gathered around him. Gilbert was explaining that
the eleven languages he spoke did not include the
seventy-eight Chinese dialects he also had at his command.

Jingee groaned inwardly. Did he have to hear this story
again?

A tall woman in a grey silk gown asked, "How do you
plan your future with such extensive gifts, Mr. Gilbert?"

Jingee held his breath as he waited for Cheng-So Gilbert's reply. It had been no secret aboard the *Huma* that
Horne was considering recruiting a new Marine into his

special squadron. Granted, Cheng-So Gilbert had been helpful in the escape from Whampoa, but was being able to imitate the warble of Chinese waterfowl qualification enough to become a Bombay Marine?

A half-smile lighting his moon face, Cheng-So Gilbert answered, "Captain Horne is helping me to achieve my lifelong ambition. You see, I recently had the privilege of serving Captain Horne and his Marines . . ."

Jingee felt the earth begin to open beneath his feet.

". . . and Captain Horne has generously promised to help me secure passage on the first Indiaman sailing for England," went on Gilbert, "as well as to provide me with introductions to find employment in London. To work in England has always been my dream."

Jingee's devotion to Horne increased a hundredfold.

Lothar Schiller escaped from a clutch of English clerks and their wives. Wiping the perspiration from his forehead, he looked round the parlour for an escape route. He wanted to leave Rose Cottage and go back to the *Huma* where he was sleeping at present. Tomorrow promised to be a big day for Schiller. He was due to give a report to Commodore Watson at Bombay Castle.

Horne had assured Schiller that he should not be nervous about the coming meeting. The report Schiller had given to Governor Pigot at Fort St. George had been the important one, and the Governor had praised him for surrendering the *China Flyer* to the Bombay Marine at Kam-Sing-Moon. In recognition of his written testimony against George Fanshaw, Pigot had cleared Schiller of any criminal charges for his part in the commandeering of the Company frigate. As far as Fanshaw's future was concerned, nobody expected the Chinese to release him in the near future from Canton's Dragon Prison. Pigot had received notification from the Manchu that they were detaining Fanshaw in connection with illegal trading in China.

What is my future? Schiller wondered as he stood lost in the crowd of guests. *Will Horne persuade Commodore Watson to accept me as a Bombay Marine?*

The excitement he felt about the prospect of joining Horne's unit was only matched by the exhilaration he had felt twelve years ago when, at the age of thirteen, he signed to fight with Maurice de Saxe.

Maybe his career would prosper more as a Bombay Marine than it had on the battlefields of Europe. He hoped so. Horne was a decent man. Schiller looked across the parlour, smiling to himself when he saw that Horne was also a man with more than duty in his mind.

"I do not intend to bore you with my history, Miss Harkness."

"Would you rather hear about the piano recitals I have attended in Bombay during the last two months, Captain Horne? My teas with the Catchpole sisters? The market-place where Elvira Schoenbrauer suggested I might find artist's charcoal?"

"Your voyage out must have been adventurous."

"My only adventure was trying to avoid the companionship of a perfectly dreadful young officer, Lieutenant Tree."

"Tree?" The name was familiar to Horne. "Do you know if his name was Simon Tree?"

"Oh, dear!" Emily Harkness blushed prettily. "Lieutenant Tree's a friend of yours, Captain Horne?"

Horne laughed. "I wouldn't call him a friend, Miss Harkness. We both sailed aboard the merchantman, the *Unity*, last year. The captain had been wounded and his first lieutenant taken ill. Tree was responsible for—"

Horne stopped, realising that the attractive young lady

had relaxed him enough to do something he seldom did, divulge details of past voyages.

Bending his head, he said, "It was nothing, Miss Harkness. Your marketplace stories are far more interesting, I'm sure."

"No, don't stop, Captain Horne. Pray continue your story."

Horne regretted he had divulged as much as he had. "It was nothing, Miss Harkness."

Emily Harkness angled her head, asking with a twinkle in her pale blue eyes, "Why do men's secrets seem darker than women's?"

"If such a thing is true, it is not necessarily an asset."

Emily Harkness smiled, dimples forming on her sun-bronzed complexion. "Excuse any boldness, Captain Horne, but for a military man you are refreshingly . . . modest."

"Perhaps modesty is no more than a form of boldness, Miss Harkness."

"Is the reverse true, Captain Horne? Can boldness be interpreted as disguised modesty?"

"Forgive me, Miss Harkness. My mind's gone slow in the company of men at sea. You're too sharp for me."

"I think I should like a life at sea, Captain Horne. But certainly not in His Majesty's Navy or the Company's Maritime Service. No, I'm certain I would suffocate in all those heavy uniforms, not to mention being obedient to endless regulations and rules."

Horne smiled, thinking of accusations levelled at the Bombay Marine.

Emily Harkness appraised Horne's gold-encrusted frock-coat. "Your uniform is indeed splendid, Captain Horne, but must you wear it every day?"

"Seldom ever, Miss Harkness. Only in Bombay and on official calls of duty. There's a rumour that a Bombay

Marine looks no better than a wild buccaneer."

"How wonderful! I approve!" Her laugh was crystal-line. "I shall have to speak to my uncle. Inquire if he can enlist me as a Bombay . . . Buccaneer."

The pejorative term did not sound offensive coming from her pretty lips. Horne laughed at himself for being forgiving with someone so attractive as this spirited young lady standing in front of him.

She asked, "Do you ever recruit new Marines to this exciting life you lead, Captain Horne?"

Deciding to let her interpret his answer however she chose, he replied, "I'm seriously considering someone at this very moment, Miss Harkness."

The instant blush encouraged Horne to believe that Emily Harkness understood his feelings for her.

GLOSSARY

BRAHMIN—The highest Hindu caste

CHAPATI—Flat, disc-shaped Indian bread

DHOOLIE—A covered litter

DHOTI—Loin-cloth

DUBASH—Literally "Two languages," hence an interpreter or secretary

DUNGRI—Blue Indian cotton cloth

FERINGHI—Foreigner

KSHATRIYA—The second highest and Hindu warrior caste

PANCHAMA—Literally, "the fifth," people outside the four Indian castes

PANKRATION—Ancient manner of Greek combat, forerunner of Japanese Karate

PUNKAH—Overhead fan operated by rope

SUDRA—People below the Hindu high castes

TOPIWALLAH—Literally, men with hats; hence, foreigners

VAISYA—The third Hindu caste, the powerful merchant class